Let the Music Begin . . .

I turned away from the people who were staring at me, and started to play, "Oh, when the saints—" Not real loud. I didn't want to scare anybody. Aaron joined in, sounding soft but squeaky, and then Lenny blasted out, vibrating like he was plugged in. . . . We did it once together and then I nodded to Lenny. He played a good, loud chorus, clowning and jumping around, and pretty soon everybody was grinning at him. He finished with a big bow, turning around to face all the people. . . .

Dial Leroi Rupert, DJ

Jamie Gilson

illustrated by John Wallner

AN ARCHWAY PAPERBACK
Published by POCKET BOOKS • NEW YORK

An Archway Paperback published by
POCKET BOOKS, a Simon & Schuster division of
GULF & WESTERN CORPORATION
1230 Avenue of the Americas, New York, N.Y. 10020

Published by arrangement with Lothrop, Lee & Shepard
Company, a Division of William Morrow & Co., Inc.
Library of Congress Catalog Card Number: 79-4662

ISBN: 0-671-56099-9

First Pocket Books printing March, 1981

10 9 8 7 6 5 4 3 2

AN ARCHWAY PAPERBACK and colophon are trademarks
of Simon & Schuster.

Printed in the U.S.A.

IL 4+

FOR JEROME GILSON, J.D.

Contents

1

Prince Albert in a Can

The equator is hot, but I bet Evanston was a whole lot hotter that Wednesday morning last July. Things started out innocent enough. I was digging worms under the old silver maple in my backyard so I could go fishing in Lake Michigan next morning. The sweat was dripping into my eyes.

A big fat night crawler had just stuck his head out of a clump of dirt when the telephone rang. I grabbed him and flicked him into the coffee can, rubbed the sweat away, and sprinted into the kitchen. I stuck the can in the sink and wiped my hands on the seat of my shorts.

"Mitch McDandel," I answered. "Talk." My mother would have zapped me for that one. But just the day before, I'd heard this great phone call on Leroi Rupert's show. He's this crazy WOGR DJ that I listen to a lot, and he was taking requests on the air. "Leroi Rupert," he said. "Talk." It knocked me out.

1

The guy calling me sounded pretty excited, but his voice was long-distance fuzzy. "Mitchell McDandel, this is your lucky day! You have just won an all-expense-paid, two-week trip to Disneyland!"

"No kidding?" I yelled. The heat must have really been getting to me. I couldn't remember what contest I had entered. They don't give things like that away for nothing. I watched one of the worms wiggle his tail, trying to burrow into the dirt. Then it came to me! For sure it was that new recipe I had entered in the Mother Nature Frozen Yogurt contest the month before. "Take a quarter cup of frozen vanilla yogurt," I had written, "squash it between two round graham crackers, and call it 'Yo-Yo Yogurt.'" I knew that would win it.

"Hey, that's great!" I said. "When do I go?"

"Would you believe second Tuesday of next week?" the voice answered, sounding clearer and a lot younger. Then the laughing started. "Hey, Mitch! You really believed me, didn't you?" More laughing. Ha. Ha. Funny. Why did I fall for it?

"Lenny Barker, that was the pits," I said, mad that he'd got me. "Anyway, you didn't fool me. You couldn't fool *me* with that fake voice."

"Come on, you're a pushover," Lenny said. "Whatcha doing?"

"Digging worms," I said, glad to change the

subject. "I'm going fishing out on the pier to-morrow morning at five o'clock."

"No kidding? Listen, remind me to tell you my worm joke. It's a killer." Lenny knew more jokes than anybody. He was, you know, always clowning around. I even heard him give a book report once on a joke book. It was a riot. "How come you're going fishing at dawn?"

"It's the only time you can sit out there without melting," I told him.

"Yeah, it's hot. Ninety-eight degrees. Leroi Rupert just said. Listen, we've got air-conditioning here. Want to come over?" Lenny asked.

The cool sounded good. There wasn't even a breeze moving our kitchen curtains. They had orange and yellow flowers and it made me sweat just to look at them. "What do you wanta do, though?" I asked Lenny, poking my finger at a fat night crawler. It was lying on top of the hot dirt, looking dead.

"I don't know. Just come. We'll make some more phony phone calls."

"That's no fun." I wasn't going to make somebody else feel like an idiot. "Let's go to the pool. It won't be so bad underwater."

"It's wall-to-wall kids."

"We could go to the beach." I could almost feel the cool water lapping at my ankles. Or was that a mirage?

"Come on," vetoed Lenny. "The sand fries

your feet, and when you get to the lake it's fifty-eight degrees. Come on over, we've got a ton of root-beer Popsicles in the freezer."

"You know I don't eat that junk." My mom says it has refined sugar that rots your teeth and makes you hyperactive. But it did sound cool. And I was dripping hot. "OK," I told him. "OK, I'll see you in a few minutes."

"Mitch, hold on!" he yelled. "I just wanted to ask you one thing. Would you have believed me if I'd said you'd won a round trip to Paris?"

I hung up on him.

Just as I was getting ready to lock the door, the phone rang again. "Mitch McDandel," I answered. "Talk!"

There was a long pause at the other end. "Listen, Mitch," said a voice I knew right away. "I'll talk. And you will listen. You answer oir phone like that again and you'll spend your July afternoons working down here in the stockroom instead of free as a breeze. You hear me?"

"Sure, Da," I said. "Sorry. I was just horsing around."

"Don't horse around on the phone, friend. Now, why don't you get out and ride your bike down to the beach? I was just calling to tell you that your mother and I will bring something home from the store, so don't worry about supper. It's too hot to cook."

"Great!" I said, wiping the sweat off the tip

4

of my nose. "I already steamed those three artichokes. So could you bring some lemon to squeeze on them?"

"Fine," he said. "See you around six-thirty," and he hung up. I got off easy.

My mom and dad own this health food shop in Evanston. Sunshine, they call it. They sell everything: vegetables that are grown without chemicals, stuff made without preservatives and dyes, meat from cows and chickens that haven't been shot up with hormones, and even face creams and junk like that made from avocados and cucumbers. They started Sunshine when I was just a baby and I mostly grew up in it.

That summer we'd made a deal about my working. I had to be in the shop in June and August, but I could stay home all of July and fool around all day, as long as I fixed supper so we could all eat about six-thirty. It worked out pretty good. I'd been to all the cooking classes my mom ever gave at Sunshine, so for twelve years old I could fix a pretty good meal.

I drank a big glass of cold pineapple-coconut juice, put the worms in the refrigerator, dragged my bike out of the garage, and started tooling up the street toward Lenny's house. I wished my bike had gears so I could take the hill easier. Pumping was hot.

"Hey, where you going, man?" I heard from the curb.

"Going crazy. How 'bout you?"

"Same." It was Aaron Colby from down the block. Aaron's the shortest kid in our class, which is maybe why he's so shy with strangers. He wears his hair in this big Afro because he thinks it makes him look taller. Sometimes we fish together mornings. Once he caught this monster coho salmon and our families all had some for supper. I broiled it and served it with dill sauce.

"I'm going down to the stationery store," he said. "Gonna get some long balloons and see if I can learn how to twist up those balloon poodles. My dad says maybe I could earn some money doing them for little kids' parties."

"How much could you charge to blow balloons at a birthday party?" I got off my bike and started walking along.

"You got me," he said. "I need a *lot,* though. See, last week I bought this classy yellow fiberglass skateboard with all my saved-up birthday and baby-sitting money. Anyway, then I left it in the yard Friday afternoon and some kid stole it. It was a beauty," he said. "My dad told me if I want another one, I gotta earn the money." He pulled out a thin wallet and showed me he only had one dollar in it. "And I got ninety-four cents in my pocket. You know how much good skateboards cost?"

"Look," I told him, "I'm on my way to

Lenny's. Come on with me and we'll both go with you." Lenny lives in a second-floor apartment near Randall University here in Evanston, where his dad teaches oboe. His mom's a librarian there at the music school.

I chained my bike under his back porch and we climbed the back steps up to the kitchen door. Lenny didn't answer the bell, so we banged on the door and looked in the window. Lenny was talking on the telephone. He waved at us.

When he finally opened the door, my sweat turned to ice, the inside air was so cold. WOGR was blasting out at about fifty million decibels. "And it's one o'clock on this supernaturally steamy Wednesday afternoon," Leroi Rupert was shouting. In the background you could hear weird music that sounded like it was from outer space, and then, "Only two more days on this earth till the thrilling, chilling, WOGR-Park District jazz bash at Bennett Bowl in Evanston. And you'll win two free tickets if yours is the thirteenth call at 123-2323. Starting right NOW. Hey, dial Leroi Rupert, DJ, at 123-2323."

"You guys come on in," Lenny said. He was chewing on a root-beer Popsicle and I guess it was the humid weather that made his blond hair curl up in little springs all over his head. I heard his mom say to him once, "Leonard, you *look* like an angel. Why can't you *act* like one?"

7

"I've got some really great calls lined up," he went on.

"Calls? You calling cool Leroi?" Aaron asked him.

"No. I already tried twice today. I think it's fake anyway." He squashed his hand down on top of Aaron's head, flattening his hair. "Hey, Short, I bet I'm a foot taller than you," he said. Aaron narrowed his eyes like he was about to get mad, but Lenny went on, not even noticing. "Let's make Prince-Albert-in-a-Can calls."

Aaron's face went blank, as if Lenny was talking French.

"Like last night," he said, "my dad was telling me about all the ones he used to make when he was a kid. He lived in this little town where he used to call the drugstore and say, 'You got Prince Albert in a can?' Prince Albert is the name of this tobacco in a can, see. And when the guy would say, 'Sure do,' my dad would yell, 'You better let him out!' And then he'd hang up. He did 'Is your refrigerator running? Well, you better run out and catch it,' too."

"Are they supposed to be funny?" I asked him.

"Sure, they're funny," he said. "My dad said they were a riot. That one I did on you was funny." Lenny grinned like he was going to tell Aaron the Disneyland Special he did on me, but he flashed a look at me and changed

8

his mind fast. "I'm gonna try one on Miriam right now," he went on. "She's at work. You guys listen on the extension in the kitchen. This is gonna be good."

Lenny's sister Miriam was sixteen. She had a job as a mother's helper in this madhouse with two sets of twins. The oldest kids were six years old and the youngest ones were about two months.

Aaron held the phone and we both listened. *Burrrrrrng, burrrrrrng,* we could hear the phone ringing. Miriam answered, very crisp and proper, "Alger residence." In the background the kids were yelling their heads off.

"Hello, Miss, this is the phone company," Lenny said, in this low fake voice. "We are working on the telephone wires near your house. Do not, I repeat, *do not* answer the phone again within the next half hour or the person on the other end of the line will be blasted with forty thousand volts of electricity. Thank you." Then he hung up and dialed again. "Wait'll you hear this!" he yelled. The phone rang again. *Burrrrrrng, burrrrrrng, burrrrrrng.*

"Alger residence," Miriam said on the other end.

"Aarrrrrrrgh!" Lenny screamed. "Eyeeeeeeeegh! Yaaaaarrrg!"

"Lenny," Miriam said, laughing. "You're very funny. But enough's enough. I'm trying

to tuck two shrieking infants into their cribs."

"How'd you know it was me?" Lenny asked her. He sounded pretty disappointed.

"Intuition," she told him. "Look, Leonard, why don't you go outside and do something constructive. Hang up quick or your toenails will fall out." And they both hung up.

Aaron and I looked at each other and laughed. "One point for Miriam," Aaron said.

Lenny strolled back into the kitchen, shrugged his shoulders, and said, "My sister's too smart, that's all." He turned the radio up.

"123-2323, WOGR, 1440 on everybody's AM dial. Don't move," Leroi Rupert said, changing to his mad mystery-man voice. A dungeon-sounding door slammed shut. "Memorize this message and I will release you. . . ." He did that kind of stuff sometimes before he played a commercial. Probably about some phony acne medicine.

"Let's go," Aaron called, heading for the door.

"We're going down to Allan's Stationery Store," I yelled to Lenny, just as the telephone rang again.

Lenny held up his hand to stop us. Then he snapped off the radio. "Joe's Bar. Joe speaking," he answered. There was a pause and we could hear a loud, shrill voice on the other end. "Oh, yeah, yeah, sure, it's me," Lenny went on. His voice sounded different, though, superpolite like he was talking to a principal or his grandmother or something. "I was just kidding." This one wasn't going to be a smart-off call. "Yeah, well, *I* thought the yard looked pretty good when I left it." The person on the other end was shouting at him, *yap-yap-yap-yap-yap*. "And besides," he cut in, "you still didn't pay me for the last time. I *didn't* break that rose bush. I don't know who did, but it wasn't me. Maybe some squirrel or possum. But if I didn't do it, it shouldn't come out of my pay." The voice on the other end didn't agree, and was pretty loud about it. "No, I guess I can't prove it. But neither can you, because I didn't do it." He rolled his eyes toward the ceiling and listened a while. "Yes, ma'am. Yes, ma'am. I'll do the hedge right now. Good-bye."

He didn't slam the phone down, but you could tell he really wanted to.

"What was that all about?" Aaron asked, opening the freezer and popping an ice cube into his mouth.

"That," he said. "was Dr. Scharff." He rolled his eyes again. "Dr. Scharff, in case you want to know, is the Wolf Woman, the Creature from the Black Lagoon, and the Wicked Witch of the West. She is also my mom and dad's boss since she's head of the dumb university music department. And I have to cut her grass because Dad said." Lenny started talking faster and louder. "But every dumb time I mow her lawn she says it's wrong and she makes me cut it over and then she doesn't pay me my three dollars because she says I broke a bush or else she only pays me a dollar because I didn't cut straight rows or I left grass cuttings in the mower and it's going to rust and cost her a million dollars—or something! Dr. Scharff, you make me barf!" he ended, like an explosion.

"Yeah, well, I'm sorry," I said. Aaron and me were kind of embarrassed. It was like Lenny was going to cry. "We thought we'd go on over and get some balloons for Aaron. Can you come along?"

"No," Lenny snapped. "I'm going to sit here and foam at the mouth."

"Don't be mad at *us*," I told him. "You don't have to cut *our* grass straight."

"Look, you guys, will you do me a big favor? Will you come with me for a couple of minutes while I finish up over there?" he asked us. "She had to leave, so she won't be there. Besides, all I've got to do is trim the hedge straight. It's a whole lot easier if somebody stands back and tells you if you're clipping downhill. If my folks didn't work for Dr. Scharff, I'd—"

"Sure, we'll help," I told him. "It can't take too long." It's weird how things seem so easy in air-conditioning.

13

When we slammed the kitchen door and the heat hit us again, an afternoon of phony phone calls suddenly looked good. I left my bike locked under the porch and we started for Dr. Scharff's house, looking and feeling like three baked, stuffed tomatoes.

2

Ding-dong Ditch

The yard around the little brick house was fenced in with a row of those iron posts that look like spears. An old-fashioned metal mailbox, like the kind you see on country roads, stood right by the gate. It had a big brass nameplate on it engraved in big curly script letters, *Alvina Scharff*. And fastened to the gate was a small metal plate that said, *WARNING: These premises protected by Advance Security Patrol. Reward given for information leading to the arrest or conviction of anyone found burglarizing or vandalizing this property.*

Lenny took a key out of his jeans pocket, unlocked the padlock on the gate, and we walked in.

Lenny went up to get the clippers from the front porch. The dogs lurking at the bay window snarled at him. Aaron and I looked over the hedge that was supposed to be botched up.

15

It was as choppy as Lake Michigan in a thunderstorm. I'd have chewed him out, too.

"Say, Len, you're not—uh—planning on being a barber when you grow up, are you?" Aaron asked him, eyeing the jagged bushes.

"No," Lenny said, looking him in the eye, "brain surgeon."

"Is that hedge job your best shot or were you just trying to bug Dr. Scharff?" I asked him.

"Look, it's not all that easy. You want to try it?" He pushed the clippers at me.

I knew I could do a better job than he did. I snapped the clippers back and forth a few times to get the feel of the blades and started trimming away. Aaron and Lenny leaned back in the shade of the house.

"No sense in all of us getting hot and tired," Lenny called to me as I clipped. Green leaves were sticking to my neck and I felt like a bunch of steamed broccoli. About halfway through Aaron took over, but he was worse than Lenny. He just *slid* the blades together so the branches bent but didn't even get cut through. So I ended up clipping the whole way to the end of the row. My T-shirt stuck to my back like I'd been swimming in it, and my arms ached.

"You guys clean up the clipped sticks," I told them, "and I'll get some of that shade." I rested my forehead on the bay window to cool. Inside the living room I could see the dogs. They were mongrels—big, noisy mongrels that looked like half German shepherd and half wolf. "Ralph," they barked at me. "Ralph! Ralph! Ralph!"

"These dogs know my middle name," I yelled to Lenny.

"You want to know theirs? They're Beethoven, Brahms and Johann Sebastian Bark. There's a cat in there, too," Lenny shouted.

I cupped my hands around my eyes and looked in closer. The cat was sitting on a fancy purple sofa across from the window. Her ears were cocked forward and her tail was all fluffed out. "Yeah, I see her. Gray. Long hair. She must be hot."

"Dr. Scharff calls her Fog."

"Fog?"

"Yeah, my dad said it's because of this poem about fog coming in on cat's feet. Sounds queer to me. The cat's weird, too. She really hates the doorbell. I rang it once and Dr. Scharff told me never to do it again because it makes old Fog climb straight up the drapes."

"If I wanted to calm that cat down, first off I'd change her name to Angel or Beauty or something," Aaron said. *"Fog,* what kind of name is that?" The cat stared at us through the window without blinking, flashing her tail back and forth.

Lenny joined us, peering in. "She looks like she's listening to us. Let's stare her down."

The cat won. So we left off window-watching and put the clippers back next to the door. The three dogs were still barking.

"Let's ring the bell and run," Lenny said. "Let's ding-dong ditch."

"Nobody's there. Wouldn't be anybody to ditch," Aaron said.

"That gray fog cat's gonna climb up the drapes and sit on the curtain rod if we do," Lenny went on, starting to laugh.

"That'll teach her to stare *us* down. Ding-dong ditch!" I yelled, and pressed the buzzer three long times. We all broke up, it was so funny. The cat was yowling, the dogs were ralphing.

Lenny vaulted over a big clay pot of pink flowers on the edge of the porch. He reached down in the grass and picked up a rock the size of his fist. "Look what I found. If I ran over this thing with the lawn mower the whole machine would fly apart. Here, catch." And he threw it to Aaron. Aaron missed it by a mile and we all watched, panicked, as it crashed into one of the little windowpanes next to the door. The glass shattered and we could hear it sprinkle sharply on the floor inside the house.

Lenny groaned. "Geez, why didn't you catch it, klutz?"

"Why did you throw it?" I asked him. The three dogs, the hair on the back of their necks standing up, were baring their teeth at us.

"Let's get out of here," Lenny yelled. I

18

spun around and started to leap over the pot of pink flowers.

"Wait!" Aaron hissed, and stuck out his arm to stop me.

I grabbed him for balance. "Whadda ya—" We teetered together, hit the flowerpot straight on, and then took a nose dive into the grass. I could hear the clay crumble and feel the wet mud ooze into my sneaker.

"Geez," I heard Lenny say again.

All my breath must have been knocked out when I fell on my stomach, because I couldn't breathe. I just lay there on the ground gulping, trying to suck air into my lungs. When I finally did get a breath, it smelled like green grass and panic.

The panic was right there in front of my eyes. It was a pair of ladies' shiny black shoes with glittery stones on the toes.

"Leonard Barker," said a loud voice above the shoes, "you are absolutely incorrigible. I can't leave you alone ten minutes. I told your father I would assist you this summer by hiring you to maintain my lawn. But not only do you have virtually no gardening skills, but you bring trespassers onto my private property. And Leonard, you broke that pane of glass. I watched you, so you can't deny it."

Lenny didn't say anything.

"*You* are a vandal," she said sharply to Aaron, who was up in a second.

19

"I didn't mean it," Aaron told her in a quiet voice.

" 'Didn't mean it' stands for nothing. You've destroyed my property." The dog behind the broken window growled. "Quiet, Beethoven," she said grandly. "I'm dealing with this." Then she aimed her voice straight at me. "You! Stand up, young man."

It was the kind of voice you did what it said. Lenny should have told us you didn't ding-dong ditch even the *cat* of somebody who

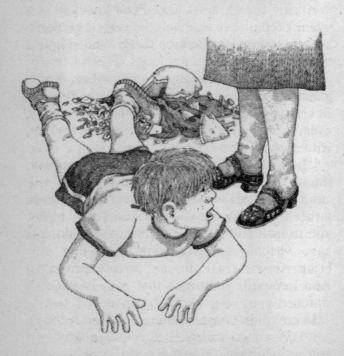

talked like that. I stood up. I was still heaving
for breath, partly because of falling into the
grass, but mostly now because I was scared.
I thought maybe if I kept gasping she'd see
how *injured* I was and feel sorry for me.

She was pretty old, much older than my
mom, and her hair was bright red, dyed red.
Her face was red, too, with the heat and because she was mad. But her dress was green
with a bunch of fancy peacocks marching
around on it. Dr. Scharff was staring me down
the way the cat did, like she knew she was
going to win. She opened her green satin purse
and took out a small silver notebook and a gold
pen.

"Your name and telephone number, if you
please," she said to Aaron. She sounded like
she thought she was the queen of Evanston,
Illinois. I figured she was just bluffing, though.
Trying to scare us. Like the cops do when you
go to the Cubs opening game on a school day.
They stop you and scare you by taking your
name, but they never call your house. Aaron
gave her his name and telephone number. She
wrote them down. Then she turned and looked
me over. "And *your* name," she said.

I sure didn't want that red-haired lady in the
peacock dress to know who I was. I couldn't
tell her my name. No way, even if I had to
take a lie detector test later. I started rolling a
few others over in my mind. George Washington? Spiderman? Clark Kent? Leroi Rupert?

"Leroi Rupert," I told her.

Aaron gasped and put his hands over his eyes. He grabbed his forehead like it was going to fly off.

"Phone number?"

"123-2323," I said, getting in deeper. Actually, since it *was* Leroi Rupert's number it really wasn't a lie, right? She wrote it all down in the little silver notebook.

This time Lenny gagged. "Dr. Scharff," he said weakly, "is there anything we can do? I mean, like . . ." His voice trailed off.

"Do? Of course there's something you can do." She put the notebook and pen in her purse and snapped it shut with a click like an exclamation point. "You can repay me. For the excellent ceramic container . . . I estimate fifteen dollars. And that is being *generous* to you. For the geraniums, with tax, I paid at least seven dollars."

"Twenty-two dollars?" Lenny gasped. "You want twenty-two dollars for a pot of flowers?"

"That's right. And a glazier will overcharge me ten dollars to repair even that small pane of glass. Prices are just frightful."

"I bet we can save the flowers," Aaron said quietly. "We didn't kill them. We just bent them a little." He reached down and packed the wet dirt together around the roots of the flowers, trying to make them stand up. They drooped, but they didn't look desperate. "See, they're hardly hurt at all."

Dr. Scharff leaned over them and looked at the pink flowers propped up in the mud and broken clay. She sighed out loud and waved her arm toward them. The sleeve of her green dress flapped like a bat's wing. "All right. If some of them can be saved, I will reduce that to twenty dollars even. Plus ten dollars for the window."

"Please, ma'am," I said, trying to remind her who had the key to her front gate. "Please, Dr. Scharff, don't tell Lenny's dad. He'd get really mad. We'll pay you."

"Yes," she said sharply. "You certainly will. But I will tell Lenny's father *and* yours—"

I gagged. This was going down the drain fast. What if she actually meant it? What if she called 123-2323 and asked for Leroi Rupert's *father?*

"—I will, indeed, inform *all* of your parents unless you repay me promptly for the damage you've done." She put her hands on her hips and looked up at the sky like she was thinking hard. "This Friday is a reasonable date, I think."

"But this is Wednesday," Lenny wailed.

"Yes," she said, "it is. This should teach you and your accomplices concern for the property of others."

"We'll have to rob a bank," I said.

"You young people need to use your wits," she answered. "And you're lazy. Leroi, I'd rather you earn this money yourselves than ask it of your parents. They broke nothing. You did. If I told them now, they'd probably just pay me themselves and you'd learn nothing. Modern parents spoil their children shamelessly. Shamelessly! However, if you haven't paid the thirty dollars by Friday, I'll be forced to call and tell them of your unfortunate behavior, and to demand compensation."

"Thank you," I said, trying not to sound too sarcastic. I could tell she expected us to be grateful to her, and look, it was a whole lot better than having her pick me up by my hair and make me call my folks. She was awful, but she could have been awfuller.

She looked over at the bushes. "Leonard, the hedge looks elegant. Why didn't you do it right the first time?" Lenny held out his hand for the money. She looked down at his palm, but didn't make a move to put anything in it. "I'll apply the three dollars to the thirty you owe me," she said. She nodded to us, walked up the steps in those sparkly black shoes, unlocked the door, and went in.

"Oh, Fog," we could hear her wail. "Baby! What *ever* are you doing up there? Come to Mommy, my precious love."

We turned and ran through the scorching heat like criminals being chased by flashing red lights.

3

What Are We Gonna Do?

By the time we'd slowed down at the end of the next block, Lenny was giggling like a TV laugh track. He couldn't run any farther. "I've got it," he kept saying. But he was stumbling along, laughing too hard to tell us what he'd got. And when he stopped, his laughing had turned into hiccups.

"I don't know about you," Aaron said, shaking his head, "but I don't see anything funny about this whole mess. Just about two hours ago, I was heading nice and innocent to buy a bag of balloons. Now, all of a sudden, I've practically got a police record."

"I've re-*hic*," Lenny started, and then tried again. "I've really got it. I know how to get the money eas-*hic*-y."

"You do? Eas-*hic*-y?" I said, beginning to feel a little better, thinking Lenny was onto something. Maybe he kept money stuffed in his pillow.

"Sure," he went on, grinning like one of those smile buttons. "You know that sign, *hic,* on the front of Dr. Scharff's gate?"

"Sign? What sign?" I asked.

"The little one that looks official," he went on. "You can't miss it. I read it ever-*hic*-y time I walk in. *Warning,* it says, *These premises protected by—*"

"Yeah, yeah, I saw it," Aaron interrupted him. "So?"

"So, I just call Advance Security Patrol, turn you and Leroi, *hic,* Rupert here in for vandalizing the property, ask thirty dollars reward, and we're home free. *Hic,* that should—"

Aaron and me tackled him at the same time, flattened him in the grass, and grabbed his feet. I picked him up by one leg and Aaron got him by the other.

"Enough!" Lenny yelled. "Stop! I give up. Geez, you guys haven't got *any* sense of humor."

Aaron was mad. "Listen, you got us into this. You're going to get us out! It's no joke to me."

I dropped Lenny's foot. "No joke to *you?* What about me?"

"You didn't even tell her your name. So what are you worried about?" Aaron asked, dropping Lenny's other foot. "She calls 123-2323 and all she gets is a snappy line from cool Leroi, whose father probably lives in Keokuk, Iowa."

"Look, you guys," Lenny said, trying to stand on his feet again. "The only one of us she really knows is me. But she knows me good. Say she says to my dad after some big music staff meeting, 'Mr. Barker,' " and Lenny started throwing his arms around and talking with this phony, high squeak, " 'Mr. Barker, your son and two young vandals, one with an *abundance* of freckles and two, possibly three, blue eyes and another with an Afro that makes him look six feet tall, have been destroying my property and absolutely terrorizing my *darling* pets and they owe me at least thirty dollars, maybe a million.' Anyway, it's gonna take my dad like four or five seconds to figure out who you are."

We all stood and looked at the ground and said nothing. The air was heavy like a hot shower.

"And there goes my new skateboard," Aaron finally said, sighing. "We're gonna have to get thirty dollars and give it to her. I don't think we can any way wiggle out of it."

"Subtract my three dollars," Lenny said, emptying out his pockets to show us all he had in them was lint. "All the money I've got, she's got."

"You know what else you got?" I asked him, using my best, most vicious snarl.

"No," he said, stepping back a little. "What?"

"Cured of your hiccups," I told him, laughing. Then I collapsed under a tree. I didn't have any laughs left.

"OK," Aaron said. "We're in this up to our eyeballs. What are we gonna do?"

"So we owe thirty. How much you got?" Lenny asked me.

"Actually, I'm loaded," I told him. "The good news is that I make two dollars and fifty cents an hour at the store." Lenny beamed. "But the bad news is that my folks put it away for my education. All I get is two dollars and fifty cents a week allowance. Mostly I spend that at the swimming pool and stuff. All I've got saved is two dollars and thirty cents. How about you, Aaron?"

"Dollar ninety-four," he said, digging his billfold out of his pocket. "But, look, I've still gotta buy those balloons. My dad said. They're seventy-five cents, plus three cents tax."

I picked up a twig and figured it all out in a patch of bare dirt at the foot of the tree.

$$\$1.94$$
$$\underline{-\ .78}\text{ balloons}$$
$$1.16$$

$$\$1.16 - A$$
$$2.30 - M$$
$$\underline{3.00 - L}$$
$$\$6.46$$

"Grand total of six forty-six," I said, scratching it out. "You suppose she'd take it in quarters over five years?"

We wandered across the street to Terman Park, dragging our debt with us. Thinking about it made us even hotter, so we took long lukewarm drinks from the water fountain. Then we stuck our heads in the bubbler and shook them out like dogs do. Across the park there were ladies playing tennis. We watched. They looked really hot. Eight crazy ladies running around in the sun.

All of a sudden Lenny shouted, "That's it! We could sell lemonade over there and make a bundle."

"Lemonade? I never broke even on a lemonade stand in my life," I told them. "The lemons and honey always cost too much. And my folks wouldn't give them to us." I sat down on a playground swing and dug my toe into the hot dust.

"You make lemonade with lemons and honey?" Lenny asked, clearly not believing a word of it. "That's stupid. It costs way too much. Besides, nobody would like it. You're supposed to make lemonade from that powder in a can."

"My mom won't let me drink that stuff."

"*You* don't have to drink it, dummy. We're selling it."

"Look, we spend all we've got for supplies and by the time we get back here," I pointed out, "the tennis players will have melted or the rain will have started or—besides, you have to be little and cute to make a lemonade stand pay.''

"You are some kind of pessimist," Lenny said, sticking his thumb over the spout and shooting me with the spray.

"Well, I've got an idea," Aaron said, sitting down in the swing next to me and rocking back and forth. "I don't know how you'll like it, but it's the only one I can think of . . . I don't know . . ." He ran his hands up and down the chain that held the swing. Finally he said, "Lenny, what do you play?"

Lenny was squirting the spray up in the air so it would rain down on him. He stopped. "Baseball, dodgeball, soccer. I can do any of that stuff."

"No, you know. I mean, your dad teaches oboe. Don't you play that? Or guitar? Or harmonica?" He stopped swinging, chewed on his lip a minute, and then said, "Listen, this probably won't work, but my dad came home from the office a few months ago—near Christmas—and he was really tickled. At supper he told us about these kids. He said they were riding on the train and playing their musical instruments. My dad said that after they played 'Jingle Bells,' they passed around a hat. They went from car to car and people kept filling the hat with money. I don't know, but he thought it was just great. He talked about it all the way through to the rice pudding.''

31

"On the train?" I asked. I hated going to Chicago on the train. I'd only been as far as Wrigley Field by myself and I sure didn't want to go shooting across the city and getting lost with next to no money. "I'd just as soon not," I told Aaron. "I don't play that good."

"Faker," Aaron said, laughing. "You looking for a compliment? You play great clarinet. You'd be lead player. And Lenny would play the—"

"This *is* gonna be a gas," Lenny said, squooshing his hands around in the mud pond he'd made with all his squirting. "I play the *piano*. What d'you suppose they'll do when I wheel our baby grand up and say, 'Lady, do I have to pay for the baby?' " He laughed. "By the way, did you know you can tune a piano, but you can't tuna fish?"

"Get serious," I told him. "What do *you* play, Aaron?"

"Violin. I'm not bad."

"Never heard you. How long you played?"

"Since October. I can play 'Twinkle, Twinkle, Little Star'—"

"Cute," I said. Babyland.

"Also Bach's Minuet in G."

"Marvelous," Lenny said, sarcastically. "You gonna get us thirty dollars for that?"

"I guess not. Forget about it," he said, and we sat there for awhile not saying anything. "We've got to do something, though," he went on. "Mitch, I've heard you play 'When the Saints Go Marching In." Maybe I could learn a violin part to that."

" 'Saints' with you, me, and old Barrel of Monkeys here singing along?" I asked. "They'd pay us to get *off* the train. No, let's think of something else."

"It's probably a dumb idea anyway," Aaron said.

"You got a better one?" Lenny asked me.

"Sell worms?" I suggested, knowing we could never dig enough.

"Worms? Sure, we could plow them up in Dr. Scharff's front yard. Hey, I never *did* tell you my worm joke," Lenny said, and he steamed into it. "There was this little kid out ice-fishing one January day, see. He'd cut this hole in the ice and he was really hauling them in. Eight, ten fish, see. When these two old guys came fishing, too, they couldn't catch a thing. Nothing, zip. So they—"

"Come on, Lenny," I told him. "Leave the jokes for later. Look, could we earn enough running errands?"

"No," Lenny said. "We couldn't." He stood up on a swing and began pumping so it looked like he was going to go over the top. "What are you gonna do?" he yelled. "Go up to the nearest house, knock on the door, and say, 'Hello there, sir or madam, whichever the case may be, you got any errands you want

33

run? We only charge thirty dollars.' They're gonna lock the door and call the police."

"Come on down," Aaron called to him. "I've got you a movable instrument maybe." He smiled. "My four-year-old sister Lucille plays it, except when she says it tickles her mouth." He took something out of his pocket and held it up for Lenny to see. "And here it is. The marvelous musical comb. All you do is wrap it in waxed paper and hum into it."

"Fabulous," Lenny said, jumping off the swing. "You know, Miriam's got one of those combs that blows your hair dry. If I used that one, I'd be the first electric comb player on my block."

"Hot Lips, they'd call you," Aaron said, laughing. "Look, maybe it won't be so bad. Everybody go home and start practicing 'Twinkle' and 'Saints,' forget the minuet, and we'll meet tomorrow morning at the Dempster train stop at . . . Listen, I can't make it before eleven-fifteen. I baby-sit Lucille every morning till eleven. But I can get there, if I have to, at eleven-fifteen."

"Eleven-fifteen it is, at the Dempster Street station," Lenny said. "Geez, it sounds like a blast."

Lenny and I walked back to his house, leaving Aaron to buy balloons. I unchained my bike and rode slowly home through the sizzling heat, wondering how Dr. Scharff would like about ten ding-dong ditches next Halloween.

Riding the Rails

"What's the trouble?" my mother asked at breakfast. "The milk's fresh."

The clumps of granola just swam there in my bowl of milk. Usually I fish out the raisins and dates, eat them first, and then inhale the rest so fast Mom gives me the old chew-every-bite-ten-times routine. But I didn't feel like it today. I put my spoon down and stared out the window. I'd just about decided that Aaron's dumb train idea was better than having Dr. Scharff on my back.

"What's on your agenda today, Mitch?" my dad asked me.

"Just gonna fool around."

"Then how about fooling around at the store?" he said, folding up his napkin and pushing away from the table. "You can grind some peanut butter for us. We're low. Lots of people making sandwiches in this weather."

"I really can't. See, Lenny and Aaron and

35

me thought we'd try to form a sort of jazz combo and fool around playing some music today. I promised them."

"Great idea," Dad said. "Glad to hear it. First-rate summer project. What do the other guys play?"

"Uh . . . Aaron plays the violin."

"Violin and clarinet?" He raised his eyebrows. "Some jazz combination." Then he shook his head like he thought I'd probably sprinkle soy sauce on my fruit salad, too.

"And Lenny?" Mom asked. "He plays the piano, doesn't he?"

"Well, uh." I shoved a huge spoonful of cereal into my mouth and started to chew very, very slow and careful. Nobody was going to get me to say that Lenny was playing the comb.

"We better get going, Sarah," my dad said. "Stop in at the store if you have any free time, Mitch."

"Have a good day now, and don't get into any trouble," my mom said, smiling. She planted a big kiss on the top of my head.

I sat around thinking about how the whole day looked like trouble. I practiced "Saints" and tried a few variations on that simpleminded "Twinkle." The kitchen was no cooler than the day before, but I hard-boiled a couple of eggs anyway, and chopped up a batch of peppers, onions, tomatoes and cucumbers for the gazpacho I was fixing for supper. When it got close to eleven-fifteen, I dragged out an old, red Cubs cap from the closet and started out for the station as slow as I could.

Lenny and Aaron were waiting for me. I was ten minutes late.

"What took you?"

"I was looking for a cap. Think this'll hold thirty dollars' worth of pennies and nickels?"

"This had better work," Aaron said. "I've only got a dollar sixteen left after the balloons." He shook his head. "And all I've done so far is pop two of them."

"Lend me a quarter, will you, Mitch?" Lenny stuck out his hand as we started into the station. "I'm broke."

"Why didn't you borrow some from your folks?" I asked him. "Wouldn't they lend you even a dollar or something?"

"They think I've still got grass-cutting money coming in. I just can't keep it, though. Whenever Dr. Dragon does pay me, I spend it. How do you think I got my great collection of comic books and bubble gum cards? Miriam lent me a dollar a couple of days ago and I blew it on a hot fudge sundae, so she laughed when I asked her for more. Listen, I'm really flat broke."

I fished out a quarter and gave it to him. My two dollars and thirty cents felt like it was dripping through my fingers.

"Hey, don't forget, you guys, we're all eleven years old," Lenny whispered as we walked up toward the cashier.

"I was twelve in June," I told him. "And you're a month older than I am."

"Shhhhh," he said, looking around to see if anybody had heard me. "Today we're eleven. You can ride half-price if you're not twelve yet. We've got to save all we can." He smiled brightly at the lady collecting fares. She glared at us like she knew, but she didn't say anything.

Evanston is the closest suburb north of Chicago. It's right on Lake Michigan. And when the train leaves Evanston for Chicago's main business district, called the Loop, it goes for a long way on these huge steel stilts above the ground. I guess it's because that way it's not so dangerous to cars and to people who are walking and stuff. Sometimes, though, it gives you a funny feeling in your stomach looking down from up there.

Except for a few trips to the baseball game, I hadn't ridden on the train. My mom and dad work all week and on Sundays we mostly go toward the country, not into the city. "You ever been on this by yourself before?" I asked Aaron.

"Once," he told me. "I went to my dad's office in the Loop this summer. And then last spring he let me go to the Cubs opener with a couple of kids from my homeroom. But I've ridden lots of times with my mom. It's not so bad."

"It's nothing," Lenny said. "I been on it lots and lots of times," he bragged as we walked up the steps to the train platform. On the way up we read the graffiti that was spray-painted on the walls. There wasn't anything good. *Elvis Lives, L. A. loves L. S., Puncho Latin Kings*, you know, stupid stuff like that.

Aaron was carrying his violin in a case, Lenny had the comb in his pocket, but I'd just brought my clarinet along plain, tucked under my arm.

Up on the platform, we sat down on what looked like old green park benches. There were signs all around advertising R-rated movies, fortune tellers and the All-New Channel Five NewsTeam. Somebody had drawn moustaches on them. And horns.

A sign behind the bench said, *These facilities for passengers only. No loitering permitted*.

"Hey, Aaron," I whispered, "do you suppose playing on the train is against the law, too?"

"I don't think so," he said in my ear. "My dad saw those other guys doing it. You know, though, I wish . . ." he started, but then he just stared down at the violin on his lap.

I got up and looked down at the tracks. They were different from regular train tracks. There were three rails. Teachers are always warning

you about the third rail because it's electric and will kill you if you touch it. It's got enough volts in it to make the trains run. Funny, I never could tell which one it was. I always expected it to be different from the others, glowing red like coals or buzzing like a neon light. People kept leaning out over the tracks to see if the train was coming. You'd have to *pay* me to do that, I was thinking, just as Lenny came up and stuck his fingers in my ribs. I jumped a foot and had to swallow hard to keep my breakfast down. Sometimes Lenny just doesn't know when to quit.

"I hear they fry two or three a year on that rail," he said, cackling like a vampire. "What would you do if your cap flew off and landed down there?"

"Very funny," I said. I moved back to where Aaron was sitting. People kept climbing the steps to the platform.

"Must be a Cubs game today," Aaron said. "Sure is crowded." The train goes right by Wrigley Field on the way to the Loop.

"When do we start playing?" I whispered to Aaron, eyeing the people who were milling around. Nobody looked like the type to throw us a dollar bill. I pulled my cap down tight.

"Later," he said, talking low, like we were plotting armed robbery.

The train squealed into the station and I pushed my way through the door with Aaron so we wouldn't get separated. "Stop shoving," the man in front of us said. The train was sticky hot. It was already jammed, with only one seat left. Lenny grabbed it. And I held onto a pole just in time. The driver must have got his training at the Indianapolis 500. A real hot dog. He was trying to see how many passengers he could deck before we got to Howard Street, the end of his line. He'd open it up full speed and then slam on the brakes just before the next stop, throwing people around. If they weren't holding on really tight they'd crash into the guy next to them or fall flat on the floor.

"Get that thing out of my face, kid," a thin man with a ragged gray beard snarled, and I tightened my grip on the clarinet.

"Hey, you guys," Lenny whispered, "our troubles are over." We looked across to where he was pointing, but all we could see were people reading their papers or trying to keep their balance. Aaron glanced at me and shrugged his shoulders.

"The *ad*," Lenny hissed loudly. "Read the *ad*." You could see all the faces lift up from their papers and look over to the poster Lenny was pointing at. It had a grinning polar bear on it, leaning back in a fancy sailboat. He was holding a big iced drink in his paw. Next to him it said, *There's Nothing Like Cold Cash for a Hot Summer. Get Fast, No-Hassle Loans for Vacation, New Car, Boat, Camper, Etc. Up to $500 on Your Signature. Lincoln*

*State Bank. Evanston. Our Most Important
Customer is You.*

"Hey, Le-roi," Lenny called, grinning. "Just
sign your name—Leroi Rupert—and we'll get
five hundred dollars for etcetera. No hassle."

I looked down at the floor rattling under me.
The faces fell back to their papers.

"Pretend we don't know him," Aaron said,
turning away.

"Howard," the conductor called. "Everybody off." Howard Street is the boundary
between Evanston and Chicago. It's where the
Evanston trains stop and the Chicago trains
start their lines. So when the doors opened
there, the three of us joined a crush of people
rushing across the platform, trying to get a seat
on the train that was heading into the city. It
must have had eight cars on it, but it was still
crowded.

Aaron and me got a seat by an open window,
and Lenny kneeled backward in the seat in
front of us so we could plan together. By then
it began to dawn on me that living through all
of that wild stopping and starting was going to
be pure bliss compared to Aaron's lunatic
combo idea. As I looked around at all the people staring out the windows or down at their
shoes or reading their papers, I suddenly realized that I was supposed to get up in front of
all of them, play the clarinet, and ask for
money.

"I don't think I can do this," I said.

43

"I don't want to either," Aaron confessed.

"We've come this far," Lenny said.

"Well, I know I can't hold the cap," I told them. "I need two hands with the clarinet."

Lenny plucked the cap off my head, tossed it in the air, and caught it on his head. "The comb only needs one hand," he said.

"You practice it?" Aaron asked him.

"Sure," Lenny said. "I played it for my dad last night. He thought it sounded great. 'You ought to go on the stage!' he told me. 'There's one leaving in ten minutes!' "

Lenny turned to look out the window, then whirled back around and yelled, "Here comes a cemetery. Hold your breath." We all sucked in. Everybody knows it's super bad luck to breathe when you go past a cemetery, but this one was two blocks long. The train crept along as slow as fresh-made peanut butter pouring. We looked down at angels and those little stone houses and tall pointed marble posts that said *ROGERS* and *SUTTER* on them. I couldn't take it that long and I snuck a breath. At the end of the cemetery, we all exploded at once.

"You cheated, Mitch," Lenny said. "I saw you. Now you're gonna have bad luck today. Geez, if you can't hold your breath that long, how can you blow that thing?"

At every stop, Lenny wanted to get up and play, but people kept pouring in—gangs of kids on their way to see the Cubs, wanting to get there for batting practice.

"Addison Street. Wrigley Field," the conductor finally announced. "No smoking on the train." Gobs of people filed out, yelling and cramming their elbows into other people's ribs. The car was about half empty. Aaron and me looked at each other, panicked, knowing that pretty soon we were going to have to play.

"Thank heavens! I thought those beastly children would *never* get off the train," a very large sweating lady behind us said to her friend. "All that yelping and screaming. It was giving me a perfectly terrible headache." I looked around. She was fanning herself with her newspaper. If we started to play now, she'd probably make a citizen's arrest.

"Let's wait a stop or two," Aaron said. So we sat and watched the buildings go by— Linda's Grocery, Carlito's Place, back porches with lines full of clothes drying, even a factory that had burned up, its water tower crashed into the top floor. A train passed by in the opposite direction, blasting us with a loud whine and hot smoky air.

Suddenly the high platform the train had been traveling along bent down toward the ground and then into the ground, and we entered the deep hole of a tunnel. I'd never been that far on the train before, to where the tracks lead underground into the subway. I didn't like it much. The lights flickered off and on a few times, and when they stayed off for about a minute it was as dark as a closet. The sound through the window got a thousand times louder as it echoed off the tunnel walls, and the smell was musty and dark like our basement after a long rain. Another train went by, and the wind whipped in our window as fast and as loud as a jet. Then our train screamed around a curve.

"Let's get off at this stop," I yelled. "Nobody could *possibly* hear us down here." I poked Lenny. "Come on, let's go." I stood up, hugging my clarinet, and scrambled toward the door. Lenny and Aaron followed. The train screeched to a stop. The doors opened in toward us like they meant to knock us down.

"Hey, kid," a man yelled. The guy who'd been sitting next to Lenny was holding up my Cubs cap. As Lenny and Aaron got off, I ran back, grabbed the cap, pulled it low on my forehead like some spy, and started for the door. But it slammed in my face with a hiss. "Pull the handle, kid," the man shouted. I didn't know what he was talking about. He pointed up to the emergency handle above the door. A sign said, *Do not pull handle except in emergency*. If I ever saw one, this was it. I pulled, the doors slid open, and I flew out onto the station platform like I'd been shot from a cannon. Aaron and Lenny stared, almost as scared as me.

Then Lenny laughed. "You almost broke off into a solo act," he said. The train screeched away, and we stood there in the damp gray tunnel, covered with noise.

I took the mouthpiece cover off my clarinet, sucked on the reed to wet it, took a deep breath, and blew as hard as I could. "Oh, when the saints go marching in, Oh when the saints go marching in, Lord, I want to be in that number, When the saints go marching in."

5

Call 123-2323.
That's 123-2323.

Lenny whipped out a big green plastic comb, wrapped it in a sheet of waxed paper, and started to hum through it with this weird, vibrating sound. The subway tunnel bounced "Saints" from wall to wall like singing in a shower. I never sounded better. Lenny grabbed the cap from my head and held it out in front of him, all the while humming and tapping his foot. A couple of people who had watched me escape from the train were clapping. A few of them even threw in coins. It didn't seem so bad after all. We got through "Saints" three times before stopping, picking up at least three dollars in change. By then a whole new set of listeners had come down the steps into the subway.

Then I noticed Aaron. He was just standing back against the wall and looking at his feet.

He hadn't even opened up his violin case. I thought maybe he was scared.

A lady chewing gum threw in a dime and said to her friend, "Aren't they cute, doin' that." They giggled and walked up the steps.

I wondered if I should tell Aaron that when you play loud you don't notice being scared. Then I decided maybe we looked so stupid, he was just pretending he didn't know us. We played the same thing through about six times and the next train still hadn't come. People were beginning to wander away or give us dirty looks. "Shall we try 'Twinkle,' " I asked Lenny, "or just go?"

"Just go," Aaron said. "I feel sick."

We pushed our way through the turnstile and climbed the steps out of the station. The sign at the top said *North and Clybourn,* but I didn't know where that was. We stood in the bright, hot sunlight for awhile. There were a lot of bars and old guys hanging out in front.

"I'm thirsty," Aaron said. He was sweating like he'd just eaten a bowl of steamy chili.

"I wouldn't go in any of those places. They'd throw you out on your ear," Lenny told him.

One of the old guys started weaving toward us, a big grin on his face. He hadn't shaved for a long time and his clothes looked like he slept in them. "A band of wanderin' minstrels," he said, and laughed like it was the punch line to a very funny joke. Lenny grabbed my arm. I

49

wasn't scared. I really wasn't. He was just an old man. But Aaron stepped back.

"I used to play the licorice stick," the old man said, getting closer. He laughed again and his laugh smelled like booze. "Lemme show ya how," he said, grinning so you could see that his teeth were the color of brown mustard. "I'll show ya." He reached out for my clarinet. I turned and ran. Lenny and Aaron were with me.

"Head down to the subway," Aaron shouted.

I turned back and looked at the old man standing there on the sidewalk. He had a puzzled look on his face. "Play me a song, will ya?" he called. "Play 'Yankee Doodle Dandy.' "

We didn't look back as we raced down the subway steps. This time we paid fifty cents each, afraid to lie about our ages. Lenny took his money out of the hat.

"How you feeling?" I asked Aaron when we got down to the platform marked *Northbound–Howard Street*.

"Better," he said. "I hate this. And it was all my idea. It sounded like so much fun when my dad talked about it."

"It's not so bad once you get started," I told him. I wondered if he'd seen my hands quivering when I jumped off the train and started blasting out "Saints." I shrugged, pretending it was no big deal. "Really—you'll see."

50

We could hear the train coming. *A-clickita-clickita-clickita-eeeeeeeeeeeeee*. By the time it pulled into the station the palms of my hands were glistening. I wiped them off on my pants real casual-like, so Aaron wouldn't notice. When the door opened, Aaron and I ran through it, yanking Lenny on board after us.

"Cut it out, you guys," he said. "Relax."

I grabbed a seat and looked over the car. It didn't look so bad for us. Mostly there were older people. I smiled at a couple of ladies who had looked up when we got on.

Aaron sat down next to me and put the violin case carefully on his lap. As he opened it up, I saw the wood gleaming inside the red velvet case. Aaron's hands were shaking. "I sure don't want to hurt this violin," he said.

Through the open windows came the scream of the train, hemmed in by the dark walls of the subway tunnel. The conductor's voice crackled over the loudspeaker. "Fullerngggg next. Change for Ravenggggg and the Bungggg to Lincnggggg Parnggggg Znggg." It sounded like he was gargling with static.

"Is that us?" I shouted to Aaron.

"I wish it was," he mouthed back. "We don't transfer till Howard, remember? That's another twenty minutes."

Lenny was starting to wrap his comb in waxed paper just as we chugged up out of the ground into the bright sunlight. The lights of

51

the subway clicked off and the train climbed up high above the ground. Lenny leaned over and whispered, "You guys, put some of your change in the hat. You got any fifty-cent pieces? When people see them, they'll think that's what everybody's giving."

"Here's a dollar thirty," I said, digging into my pocket and dumping in the last of my allowance.

"I've got forty-one cents," Aaron said. "And that's all I've got."

Lenny put the money in the cap and then rearranged the total so the big cash was on top. "Including our money, we're got four dollars and twenty-one cents," he said. "Not bad for starters."

"Let's go with 'Saints' to begin with," I said, figuring the second time couldn't be any worse than the first. "These guys haven't heard it."

"We should have a sign that says *Support Your Local Youth* or *Fight Juvenile Delinquency*," Lenny said. "I'd make one but I haven't got any paper."

As soon as the train jerked away from "Fullerngggg," we stood up and planted our feet wide apart for balance. I turned away from the people who were staring at me and started to play, "Oh, when the saints—" Not real loud. I didn't want to scare anybody. Aaron joined in sounding soft but squeaky, and then Lenny blasted out, vibrating like he was plugged in. I held up my hand to let the guys know I was going to play a chorus by myself. Nobody in the train looked mad, so I really let go. I got a little applause from the ladies I'd smiled at. We did it once together and then I nodded to Lenny. He played a good, loud chorus, clowning and jumping around, and pretty soon everybody was grinning at him. He finished with a big bow, turning around to face all the people.

Aaron was last. He was awful. The violin screeched so you wanted to hold your ears, and he didn't land on the right notes half the time. His hands were still shaking. When he finished it was pretty quiet, but this one gray-haired guy with wire-rimmed glasses gave him a big hand. Aaron peered down at the other end of the car to see who was clapping.

After we went through the whole number again together, Lenny said, loud enough that everybody could hear, "OK, now we collect! Can't expect to get entertained like that for free." He picked up the cap and started down the aisle. I followed along. Aaron put his violin in the case and came after. Lenny was reaching out with the hat and talking, even to those people who had started staring out the window like they were watching a house burn down. "Did you like us?" he'd say. "How about a little donation to a needy cause—us!" They'd kind of laugh and, more often than not, they'd put in money, too. Not dollar bills, but quarters and dimes. They thought we were pretty funny, I guess.

"They're tickled like your dad was," I said to Aaron to cheer him up.

"I never figured they'd be laughing at us like this," he said.

When we got to the other end of the car, the old gray-haired man who'd clapped for Aaron said, "How long you been playing that violin?"

" 'Bout a year October," Aaron told him, not looking up.

"You practice that piece much?"

"Not enough. Just last night."

The man closed the magazine he'd been reading and folded his hands over it. "Play anything classical yet?"

Aaron shrugged. "A Bach minuet."

"Can I hear it for a dollar in the cap?"

Aaron looked up to see if the guy meant it. He didn't look like he was making fun. He really looked interested and Aaron was just getting ready to open his case when the car pulled into the next station. "Arngggggg," the conductor announced over the loudspeaker.

After the people got off and on and the train lurched forward again, the man looked at Aaron, smiled, and nodded. Aaron got up and leaned back against the seat. He was biting hard on his bottom lip. Taking a deep breath, he started playing all by himself. And the minuet sounded good. It really did. The tone was clear, the notes were right, and the longer he played the better it sounded. When he finished, he sat down fast and started packing the violin away again.

The man clapped, and so did a lot of others. The people who'd just gotten on, though, looked at us like they thought we were bananas.

"Why are you young men doing this?" the man asked us.

"Because it's a big blast," Lenny said.

"We're doing it," Aaron said, "because we owe somebody thirty dollars. And that's the only reason why."

The guy put a dollar bill in the Cubs cap as the train began to slow down for the next stop.

Lenny grabbed the handle of the door at the end of car. "We better get going," he said, pulling hard to open it. Over the door was a sign that read, *WARNING: Do not cross between cars while train is in motion.*

"I'd wait till the train stops if I were you," the Dollar Man said. "It's a killer going from car to car on a moving train. Especially when you're carrying so much."

"I've seen people do it hundreds of times," Lenny snapped. The train stopped and Lenny got the door open at the same time.

"Thanks a lot," Aaron said to the guy, who smiled and waved good-bye.

There wasn't really any kind of walkway between the cars. We had to step from one car ledge to the next. Looking down, we could see the tracks underneath the train, and where the cars were hooked together. Alongside us, though, there were chains flapping back and forth to keep up from falling off. It was pretty scary.

Lenny was the first to reach the opposite ledge. He turned the handle and pushed open the other door one-handed. Aaron and I leaped into the next car behind him. The door slammed behind us with a heavy metal thud like a prison gate.

The car was packed. Lots of people had gotten on at this stop. It looked like the Cubs crowd again, coming to Wrigley Field from the other direction. Aaron sat down in a miraculously empty seat and, looking glum, got his violin out again. The train lurched forward.

A gang of sixteen- or seventeen-year-old guys was taking over our end of the car. One of them, wearing a T-shirt with a big *#1* on it, looked over and said to his friends, "He-ey, we're gonna have a concert. You guys show respect, now." They laughed, but I couldn't tell if they were friendly or not, so I just started to blow right away. "Oh, when the saints—"

"Wow-eeee, these guys gonna make the Top Ten," said Number One.

"Top Ten *what?*" his buddy asked.

"Top ten kids to get tossed off this train," Number One said, laughing. "And I may be the one to do it."

Call 123-2323. That's 123-2323.

Lenny grinned at him, but the grin looked pasted on. He took out the comb, wrapped it in paper, and started to hum.

"Go on, these babies tryin' to win our hearts. Ain't they cute? Imagine that. Playin' a comb. Lend me your comb, kid. I got a wave that needs rearrangin'."

Aaron had the violin in his hand, but he didn't play a note. He just stood up and started for the other end of the car. As he hurried down the aisle, his case knocked against a seat and flew open. The rosin for his bow bounced out and landed under somebody's legs. He kept moving.

Lenny and me followed along behind, playing fast and loud. Lenny never missed a beat, though. As soon as we got past the gang of kids, he held out the cap for money. You could tell some of the people were feeling sorry for us. They were throwing in coins and saying stuff like, "Now that sounds real nice. Don't you let those roughnecks tease you."

We must have gotten three or four dollars of that sympathy money. It sure wasn't because we were playing good.

Number One was following us. "Look at that. They're makin' real money." He was walking slow. And he was half smiling. But it was just because he knew we were quivering like jelly inside. In his hand, he had a little portable radio. He turned it up as loud as it would go and we stopped playing altogether.

"Fourteen forty on your dial," it blared out. "WOGR, Evanston." Then there was a blood-curdling scream, totally different from any scream I had ever heard. Leroi Rupert was saying, "Here's to chills down your spine this hot P.M. It's twelve-thirty-five o'clock, one hundred one in the shade. Must be sunspots causing this crazy weather. Lots of folks with the crazies, too. Lady just called wantin' to talk to my daddy about me and my ba-ad ways. Said her kitty cat wouldn't come down from the curtain tops. I told her my daddy didn't care for cats, least of all hers. Then she said it was *me* caused her cat to climb the walls. Now, not to say I don't got a way or two that's ba-ad, but this lady wasn't talkin' about me. Turns out she was talkin' about a kid who *called* himself Leroi Rupert, laying hold to my own glorious, glittering name."

Lenny, Aaron, and me were stunned. We turned and faced Number One, looking like the Ghostly Trio. We stood absolutely still, like our feet were stuck in Elmer's Glue.

"Turn that thing down," a man sitting next to us said. It must have been rupturing his ear-drums.

"I want that kid to call me," Leroi Rupert went on. "Listen, Leroi Rupert Number Two, you call with a code word so I'll know it's you. Just tell the name of that ceiling cat to the lovely lady with fangs who answers the phone here at WOGR, 123-2323. That's 123-2323.

And all the rest of you Draculate beasts out
there keep ringin' in your requests and makin'
plans to spirit yourselves out to the big Bennett
Bowl WOGR-Park District jazz concert tomorrow night in Evanston. I'm gonna be there
along with—'' *Click*. The man reached over
and snapped off the radio. Number One glared
at him, but he must have figured it wasn't
worth a hassle because he just stuck the radio
under his arm and grinned at us, cocky as anything.

Now all we could hear was the rattle of the
train. The three of us looked at each other.
Even Lenny seemed to have lost his cool.

"Hey, Big Time Band, you don't need *all*
the money in the kitty, do you?" Number One
asked, walking toward us slow. People started
looking out their windows like they were afraid
of seeing blood. We ran to the other end of the
car. Lenny grabbed the door handle, turned it,
and yanked it open.

A screeching wind blasted us and, with the
roar of the wheels, the din was even louder
than it had been underground. "Get the door
to the *next* car," Aaron shouted, barely making himself heard. "I don't have any hands."
He was standing there with the violin and bow
in one hand and an open case in the other.

I held my breath and pushed past him out
onto the heaving platform, my ears ringing
from the million decibels of noise. I'll never
grow up to be a stunt man, I thought. I even

doubted that I'd grow up at all. The cars were swaying and I could see the railroad ties shooting by.

"Move it!" Lenny yelled. I jumped across to the next car's platform, grabbed the door handle, threw my weight against the door, and pushed. But it wouldn't move.

"*Turn* the handle, stupid!" Lenny yelled.

"Hurry," Aaron said, desperately. The whole gang of kids hovered around Lenny and him in the doorway, one of them plunking on the violin strings, another one giving the top of Aaron's head a knuckle rub. No way we were gonna win against that gang of giants.

I finally turned the handle on the heavy metal door and shoved it wide open with my shoulder. Then I stood there inside the next car, breathing hard and holding the door open, my clarinet clenched under my arm. Aaron leaped in beside me but Lenny stayed on the opposite platform. He slammed his door fast, pulled back on the handle, and planted his feet hard on the bobbing platform, trying to keep the guys inside from following us. Number One pressed his nose flat on Lenny's window, in no hurry, but watching us close, like we were wiggling worms and he was the digger. I waited inside the next car with Aaron, propping the door open with my foot. The wind and wheels yowled.

"Get in here," Aaron shouted. "Get *in*, Lenny. You wanta get *killed?*"

61

Lenny was trying to hold the door closed with one hand and clutch the Cubs cap in the other. But I could see the door move as the kid inside started to pull it open.

"Let go, Lenny! You can't win," I screamed above the clatter.

"I can, too. But I gotta use both hands. Here, catch this." He flung the cap at me like it was a Frisbee. The train took a sudden curve, its wheels screaming. The force of the turn threw me out of the open door and toward the swinging chains between the cars. I grabbed for the safety handle to steady myself and reached for the flying cap at the same time. I got the handle. But I missed the cap. It landed on the place where the cars are hooked together and balanced there on the ledge, just an arm's length away. We could see the money inside—lots of quarters and dimes, and the one-dollar bill the gray-haired guy had dropped in. The cap full of money rested there, teetered, and when the train jerked the wind grabbed it and toppled it slowly over onto the tracks. It was gone. Our money was gone.

Number One let Lenny's door snap closed. He turned away, and even over the wind and the screeching of the wheels we could hear him and all his friends laughing.

6

Into the Cruel, Cruel World

The three of us sat on the train not saying a word, listening to the wheels click. Our money was scattered in the gravel and the trains would keep running over it all day and all night.

"Maybe the dollar bill will blow down and some kid will find it," Aaron said, rubbing his knuckles across the violin case.

"Yeah. 'Hey, look,' he'll say, 'some dope lost his money.'" Lenny chuckled.

"Very funny," I groaned.

"That's a kid who knows what he's talking about." Aaron closed his eyes.

"We'll think of something," Lenny said brightly. He snapped his fingers like he just remembered where he hid thirty dollars. "You know what?" he said. "I didn't finish that fishing joke. Where was I? Oh, yeah, these two old guys came up to the kid who caught this big batch of fish through a hole in the ice. 'How'd you catch so many, kid?' they asked him. See, they hadn't caught *anything* yet. 'Aumbuflondgluu,' the kid said. 'What's that?' the old guys asked him. 'Agbeumufwomflgul,' the kid said. Well, the old guys didn't know what to make of that, so—''

''Addison,'' the loudspeaker blared, clear as a bell. We must have gotten a new conductor at the last stop.

> ''Addison,
> Where every lad n' son
> Can watch the Cubs
> Or go to the pubs.
> Addison next.''

Everybody laughed, even us.

Lenny gave up on the joke. ''That conductor's warming them up for us. Let's try again,'' he said.

Aaron covered his face with his hands and groaned. ''I may never play again. I'm sure not going to play here.''

''Forget it!'' I told Lenny.

At Addison, most of the car emptied out. Number One strolled past with his radio. He looked in at us and winked. Creep.

''Forget *him,*'' Lenny said. ''We still haven't played 'Twinkle, Twinkle, Little Star.' ''

Aaron and me just looked out the window. I imagined the last few minutes over again in my mind, only this time I saved the cap full of money. It made me feel better for a second or two. But then I saw the change raining down on the tracks again and I groaned out loud. Must have been eight or nine dollars. Maybe more.

The conductor kept rhyming each station, like he was trying to cheer everybody up. Finally, when we got to the last stop on the line, he sang out:

"Howard Street.
Outta your seats.
And take your feets
Into the cruel, cruel world.
Last stop for everyone
Transfer to Evanston."

As we waited on the platform, I looked over onto the tracks, remembering how scared I'd been to look there before. A coffee-stained paper cup, a pencil, lots of gum wrappers, and cigarette butts littered the tracks, but no money. Not even a penny. Smart people don't go around throwing their money on train tracks. Lenny and Aaron were looking down, too. I knew what they were thinking. "I'm sorry," I told them. "I really am."

"It's not your fault," Lenny said. "I threw it with a stupid hotshot curve."

"I shouldn't have been yelling at you," Aaron said. "Besides, it was my stupid idea." And we all felt some better, but not much.

"When we get back," I said, "let's go to

Sunshine. I can call Leroi Rupert from there.''

"Geez," Lenny whispered. "I'd forgotten all about Leroi Rupert.''

''They'll give us lunch free and then maybe we can think better," I told them.

When we walked into Sunshine, I took a deep breath. The air felt cool and I liked the way it smelled, like fresh dill and lemons. It was always good.

Must have been a slow morning, though. Dad had had time to grind at least twenty pints of peanut butter and the produce was still stacked in straight rows, with lines of celery and corn on the cob separated by big ripe tomatoes. If they'd been busy, everything would have been scattered by customers who poke and squeeze.

We'd had a new shipment of herbal teas in,

too. The shipping boxes were open in front on the display. That would have been my job if I'd been working—emptying the boxes and filling in the spaces with spearmint, sassafras and camomile and stuff. Before I could even read, I used to stack them just by matching the pictures.

Mom and Dad were busy with customers, so I fixed us some peanut-butter sandwiches on stone-ground wheat bread, got some apple juice from the refrigerator case, some grapes just in from California, and then finished us off with frozen honey yogurt. It was good. Even Lenny liked it. But it didn't help me think any better.

We were standing over near the paperbacks eating the frozen yogurt when Mom finally got free to come over. "What have you boys been up to?" she asked.

"We've been practicing, Mrs. McDandel," Lenny said. "We're getting pretty good. We'll play for you sometime." He reached for a book about how to fix raw vegetables. "Say, this looks *very* good," he said. "My mom oughta get this. Mitch, why don't you go make that phone call and I'll keep your mom busy—I mean, I'll *talk* to her until you get back."

Mom gave me a funny look, but I sprinted off to the office at the back of the store. *"Tell me about health foods. Is carob as good as* chocolate? Lunch was *fabulous!*" I heard Lenny say.

Dad was waiting on a customer and Lenny had Mom's ear, so I sat down at the desk and looked at the phone. I *could* have just pretended I hadn't heard Leroi Rupert on the air. I didn't have to call him. I didn't know if he was mad or not. But he *was* Leroi Rupert, after all, and he wanted to talk to me, so I dialed him. I didn't even have to look up the number. I just punched out 123-2323. The line was busy. It figured. It took me three tries before I got through.

"WOGR. May I help you?" a cheerful voice answered.

". . . I . . ."

"Yes? Hello."

"I'd . . . I . . . I'd like to talk to Le—. I'd like to talk to Mr. Rupert, please. I'm . . . see, I'm the guy who said he was him."

"You're the fifteenth call I've had in the last hour from somebody who says they're 'the guy who said he was him.' So far, they've named the cat in question as Bubbles, Snowy, Sapphire, Al, Penny, Martha . . . Do you want me to go on?"

"Listen, does he really want to talk to me," I asked her, "or was he just kidding over the air?"

"If you're the one, he said to put you right through."

"Did he sound mad?"

"He sounded like Leroi. Leroi never sounds mad mad. Crazy mad, sure. Mad mad, never. What's the cat's name?"

"Fog."

"You got him." I could hear the phone ringing.

"Talk!" Leroi answered.

"Fog's on the line. I feel like I'm in a spy movie," she said, laughing.

"So, Fog, how you doing?"

"Fine, thanks, I . . . I mean, my name's not Fog, it's . . . Say, I'm not on the radio, am I?"

"No, Fog, I wouldn't do that to you. Not after what you've been through."

He was psychic, Leroi Rupert was. All that razzle and weird music. He didn't need it. He could read *minds*. Over the telephone. I grabbed the phone with both hands to steady myself. "How'd you know what I've just been through?"

"Know? I talked to your trouble on the phone for ten minutes trying to tell her that neither my mother or my father were going to pay for her geraniums. I think twenty dollars for those flowers is robbery, by the way. You think she's making money off the deal?"

"Look, I'm really sorry. But, see, when she asked me my name and she was going to write it down and call my dad she seemed so mean and yours was the first good name I thought of and . . ."

70

"Hold it! I know what you're saying. She sounded mean to me, too."

I leaned back in the chair and put my feet up on the desk. "We were out just now trying to make the thirty dollars for the flowers and the glass. We were doing pretty good but—"

"I hate to tell you this, Fog," Leroi Rupert cut in, "I sure do. But the total's up to fifty dollars. She had to take her cat to the vet today—for its nerves."

"You're kidding." I dropped my feet off the desk.

"Would I kid a Leroi Rupert?"

"No, no, I guess not. Fifty dollars, though! That's like a million. I was just gonna tell you, we lost everything we had this afternoon."

"We?" he asked. "Oh, yeah. She told me there were three of you guys."

"Three of us. Right. Lenny and Aaron and me, we went on the train to Chicago today, see." And I told him the story—how we played and collected, how we heard him on the kid's radio and about the gang of guys, and how we ran and opened the doors between the train cars and dropped the whole thing on the tracks. "So now we've got nothing. Nothing but trouble."

Leroi Rupert didn't say anything for a second. Then he said, "You played *what* on the subway?"

"We played 'Saints.' You know, 'When the Saints Go Marching In.' "

"No, I mean what instruments?"

"Oh, that. Violin, clarinet, and comb."

"Kid, I believed your story up to that point. But now, I hate to tell you, but I think you're jivin' me."

"Would I jive another Leroi Rupert?" I asked him.

He laughed. "No, I guess you wouldn't. What's your name, Leroi Fog?"

"Mitch McDandel."

"You live in Evanston?"

"Yeah, my folks own Sunshine on Main Street."

"Sunshine Health Foods? No kidding?"

"Yeah. You *know* Sunshine?"

"Know it? I live on their peanut butter."

"I *grind* it!" I shouted. "I *grind* the peanut butter. That's me!"

He laughed like he thought the whole mess was the funniest thing he'd ever heard. "Look, Leroi Mitch Fog McDandel, I've got an idea. I want you and your musician buddies to come up here to the Lincoln State Bank Building, where our studios are. I want to talk to you."

"*Now* you want us?"

"Now, if you can cut it."

"Sure. I guess, sure. OK, Mr. Rupert."

"Leroi. Everybody calls me Leroi. And listen, bring your instruments. I've got to run. I'm *coming*," he shouted to somebody. "Just play cart four-thirty-one, the new backward scream.'' Then he whispered into the phone, ''Avoid cats,'' and hung up.

I strolled back in front where Lenny was telling my mom and dad every joke he knew, practically standing on his head. ''Anyway,'' he was saying, ''these old guys asked the kid for the *third* time, 'How come you're catching fish and we're not?' Well, the wind was blowing, see, the snow was falling, and everybody's feet were turning blue because of the ice. First the kid said, with his mouth clamped shut, ''Ahkeebuuuuwuuuuamhm.' But then when the old guys wouldn't go away, he looked at them kind of mad, screwed up his face, spat out—*patoooooeeeeeeee*—and then said *very* clear, 'I keep my worms warm.' ''

Dad went off chuckling to ring up somebody's safflower oil and whole-wheat spaghetti. Lenny and Aaron turned away laughing to talk to each other.

Mom leaned over to me. ''I think Lenny's mother lets him eat *much* too much sugar,'' she said. ''I never saw a more hyperactive child. He's almost hysterical.''

''Yeah,'' I said. ''Almost. He eats tons of root-beer Popsicles.''

''Yuck!'' she said. Then she turned to Lenny. ''By the way, your mother called and wanted to know where you were. I said you were all playing your music somewhere. 'Music?' she said to me. 'You mean that *comb?*' At least it sounded like she said comb. I've been trying to figure out what it really was. It wasn't drum or horn, was it?"

"No, it was closer to comb," Lenny said. "Look, I'll call her back real soon. But we gotta be going now."

"Mitch, who were you calling, hon?" she asked, and I was just about to answer, "Weather. I wanted to find out what the temperature was," when this really pregnant lady came rushing in. She was wearing one of those stupid T-shirts printed with *Baby Inside,* and an arrow pointing down.

"I'm double-parked and I need a pound of cracked wheat and four ounces of rose-hip tea," she said, out of breath. Mom dashed off to help her.

"We're having gazpacho for supper, Mom. See you at six-thirty," I shouted, as we headed for the door.

"OK, fine," she called back, smiling at the customer like she was going to brag to her about teaching me to cook. Probably she'd tell her that *especially* if it's a boy, she should teach Baby Inside how to cook. She says it's the best thing she'll ever do for me. "Enjoy." She waved. "Don't get into any trouble."

As soon as we got outside, I told Lenny and Aaron that Leroi Rupert wanted to see us all right away, so off we went. It must have been a two-mile walk to the Lincoln State Bank Building, but the clouds had covered the sun and we stopped once in an air-conditioned drugstore to cool off. It wasn't so bad. As we walked, I told the guys the story of Leroi's run-in with the Cat Woman.

"Fifty dollars!" Aaron moaned. "I'll *never* get my new skateboard! I can't ask my dad for money, not that kind of money. I get three fifty a week for baby-sitting Lucille. I'm gonna have to pay my share in installments." He kicked a beer can so hard, it bounced half a block.

"Everybody keep your eyes down," Lenny told us. "Maybe we'll find some money laying in the street or on the sidewalk. I found a two-dollar bill once." He started across the street with his eyes scanning the gutters, when all of a sudden a car screeched to a stop in front of him. A guy leaned out and said, "Hey, kid, you trying to get yourself squashed like a to-mato?" So we all kept our eyes up and walked slowly on.

"What does Leroi Rupert want to see *us* for anyway?" Aaron asked, having second thoughts. "*You*'re the one who used his name."

"Got me. He didn't make it sound like we were turning ourselves in or anything like that."

"Maybe it's a trap," Lenny said, always thinking positive. "I know! Dr. Frankenstein Scharff is there with Advance Security Patrol and they want to get our confessions on the air."

The Lincoln State Bank is the tallest building in Evanston. It's got a big air-conditioned lobby that's marble and cool, with a dancing fountain that we'd have gone wading in if we dared. The directory listed WOGR on the thirteenth floor. Good old Leroi.

We got in the elevator, pressed thirteen, and up we went, so fast we had to hold our stomachs. Straight up to another world, another planet: Ogre, Leroi Rupert, and the backward scream.

7

On the Air

Number thirteen lit up on the little screen and the elevator doors slid open. Aaron, Lenny and me stepped out into a lobby that glowed with pink light. There were green plants all around, but no real sunlight anywhere to keep them alive. A pretty blonde lady with enormous blue-rimmed glasses sat in a glass booth facing the elevator. She glanced up from the phone call she was taking, covered the mouthpiece and whispered, "With you in a minute." Behind her there was a big silver and red sign that said, *WOGR, Serving Chicagoland.* Shiny autographed pictures of all the WOGR disc jockeys smiled down at us. Leroi Rupert was in the middle. He was wearing a monster mask for a hat, the warty nose drooping down over one of his eyes. And he had a wild, wild grin. I didn't remember seeing him before, but I guessed he wouldn't have been wearing the hat at Sunshine.

Four speakers were vibrating with what I decided must have been on the radio right then, "WORGrrrrrrrrrr! TONIGHT! OLD TIME RADIO THEATER . . . with the THRILL of the PHANTOM . . . the CHILL of the GIANT GREEN GHOST. TONIGHT at TEN on . . . OGRErrrrrrr."

"Hello," the lady at the desk said, hanging up the phone. When she smiled, I noticed she didn't have fangs at all. "What can I do for you gentlemen?" she asked. Aaron and Lenny looked at me.

"I'm . . . I'm . . . Fog, I guess," I told her.

She giggled. "I'm disappointed," she said. "I was hoping for a cloak and dagger, but I guess cutoff jeans and a T-shirt will do."

"Well, Leroi Rupert always says *you* have fangs."

"I had them filed down. They kept hitting the phone." She dialed and said, "There are three fog men here to see you. Musical fog men, I judge, unless that violin case really has a submachine gun in it." Aaron looked down and laughed nervously. "OK, Leroi, I'll bring them back," she said. "Three disenchanted fans coming right up." She hung up and the phone rang. She let it ring.

"Do we really get to go back and see where he broadcasts?" Lenny asked her.

"He's about to go on the air," she said, "but I'm going to take you back to the control room so you can watch. You think you'd like that?"

"Sure," Aaron said, quietly. "We listen all the time."

"Listening's different from looking," she said, flipping her hair back over her shoulder. She led us down a hall lined with regular-looking offices. "Here we are. Watch your feet." We took a big step up into the control room, this really small space with one big glass wall, and floor-to-ceiling shelves of little black plastic boxes. A bald guy was sitting hunched over a panel of dials and knobs. He glanced at a digital clock that was flashing out time by the seconds, then turned and looked at us as if he couldn't imagine what we were doing there.

"This is Marty Bowen," she said. "He's Chief Engineer." Marty Bowen scowled like he thought *we* were chief pains.

"Listen," she told him, these are three very important people. Leroi wants to talk to them as soon as he gets off the air. They're his Public. If you've got a minute, tell them how all this stuff works. My phone's ringing off the hook." She turned and ran like she was in a marathon.

Marty Bowen looked like a crumpled piece of paper. His face was wrinkled, his clothes were wrinkled, and he sat scrunched up over his board of dials. Next to him there was a big six-foot tape recorder, but nothing was going around on it. And there were two empty turntables for records. "Don't touch anything," he said, without looking at us. We stood still with

79

our hands at our sides, watching, while he wrote something down on a clipboard in front of him. Then he turned around to us in his revolving chair.

"I wouldn't have Michelle's job for anything," he said. "Every time Leroi gives the number, her phone rings like blazes. Just before I put this last bit on, he gave it." He pointed through the big glass window into the next room.

We looked through the window at the guy he was pointing at.

"Who's that?" I asked.

"The one and only," he said.

"Leroi Rupert?" we all three gasped at the same time.

"None other." He laughed. "Everybody comes up here's surprised."

We stared, all three of us. I'd always pictured him huge—six feet eight with eyes like he'd just stuck his finger in an electric socket, eyes like they could zap you.

"Geez," Lenny whispered, "Leroi Rupert, DJ! I thought he was a little guy with long sharp fingernails, didn't you?"

"Yeah," Aaron said. "He looks *wrong*."

The engineer laughed again. "The *real* Leroi Rupert," he said.

Leroi Rupert could have been somebody's *father*. He must have been thirty-five at least, a big, almost fat—OK, more than almost fat— black guy with no monster mask on his head,

straight eyes, straight teeth, and he was wearing a blue-striped dress shirt with a *tie*. He'd pulled the tie down so it was loose from his collar, but he was wearing one all right. In front of him on this desk was a living-room kind of lamp, a stack of papers, a telephone, and a long microphone that looked like an ice-cream cone. He was wearing an enormous set of earphones. But Leroi Rupert didn't look weird or nutty at all. He looked *normal*.

He glanced up from what he was doing and waved. The music stopped and we could hear his voice for the first time. It was him all right. "Your ear's been crazy-glued to 'Hubris,'" we could hear him say. "It's the newest single by Equinox, gonna be top big gigantean on the charts. The Morton High Jazz Band'll be playing around with their vision of 'Hubris' tomorrow night at the Bennett Bowl Bash. Only a dollar a head. Bring yours and somebody else's, too." He pointed to the Chief Engineer who grabbed a little box, stuck it into a machine next to him, and a Morgan Ford commercial began to play over the air. It had hardly started, though, when Leroi interrupted it and we could hear his voice in the control room. "Marty, give me cart 2176, and then just segue into 1540. And get out the backward scream, will you? It drives them up the wall out there. Hi kids, I'll be with you in a minute." The sound clicked off and we heard the last of the car-dealer commercial over the speakers. The engineer started another one about a big two-for-one jeans sale.

"Was Leroi on the air?" Aaron asked.

"Naw, he was just talkin' to me on the intercom. Twenty-one-seventy-six is a catalog number. It tells me what he wants to play. Look for it over there." He smiled a little, like he was almost beginning to trust us. "Grab it for me, will you?"

I ran my eye along the numbers, but Lenny got there first. "Here it is," he said, handing over this plastic box.

"This here's called a cart—short for cartridge. Each one's got just one song on it. This one's an oldie, a Beatles number. It's timed to the second, see, and both Leroi and I know exactly how long it's going to run." Leroi was sitting in the studio talking on the telephone, writing something down, just like he was in a regular office. There weren't any big rubber flies hanging from the ceiling, let alone bats.

"What's *segue?*" Aaron asked. "He said you were supposed to segue."

"Oh, that. Segue's when I fade down the music and then just fade up the next song at the same time. You know, kind of crisscross them. I control the volume with these knobs here we call pots." He shrugged. "Do it all the time."

"Is there a backward scream, really?" I asked him. For the first time he looked actually friendly.

"You like that? Yeah, sound effect cart 431. Right over there in that bin. Will you get it for me? You probably heard it and didn't know what it was. I did it myself. Got Michelle to scream as loud as she could, recorded it, then played it backward and recorded it that way on the cart. Leroi can't stop using it. Eerie, ain't it?"

"Yeah," I said. "Really eerie."

"Send the kids in, Marty, will you?" Leroi called over the intercom. Marty told us to walk around to the studio door. "Don't go in if the red *ON AIR* sign's on," he yelled after us.

The sign was dark, so we opened the door a crack.

"Come on in," Leroi Rupert said. "Watch out for the quicksand." I pushed the heavy door open and we walked in quietly and lined up against the wall. We couldn't believe where we were. And who was just a few feet in front of us.

"Vell, prisoners, you got any last vurds before ve blindfold you for the firing line?" Leroi Rupert said to us in a thick German accent. We started to laugh, but he held his hand up for us to keep quiet. The sign by the control-room window turned red. *ON AIR*, it read. I was afraid to even breathe. My nose started itching like crazy, though, and it felt like my August hay fever was going to begin in July.

"Honored friends, rabid bats, and gargoyles," Leroi said mysteriously, "I have a

84

guest in the studio today." I felt my face flush. What if he asked me to say something? "It's a thirteen-year-old . . . cyclops who just flew in from Transylvania and boy, are his arms tired. He's got flies on his fleas, scabs on his knees, and braces on his splendid fangs." He paused and glanced at us. "Coast in around the microphone, Cy, and greet the group hanging on the radio wires." I *wouldn't* say anything, I told myself. He couldn't make me.

But he didn't even look at me again. He pointed to Marty Bowen, took his earphones off, and held them out so we could hear what was going on over the air. It was the backward scream starting off soft and high and getting louder and louder. *KeeeeeeeeeEEEEEEE*. Crazy. But we didn't say a word.

"Three-thirty in this world," he went on. "I'll zap back in tomorrow at ten and take a request or two. And don't forget to get out the keys and unlock the gang for Friday night jazz at Bennett Bowl. Meantime and space, it's Leroi Rupert here oozing away into the thin green ozone. . . ."

ON AIR flicked off and he turned around to us and smiled. "I considered playing a fabulous buzzing doorbell, but I didn't want you climbing the walls. OK, which one's Fog?"

I held up my hand like I was in class.

"Ah, of course, the clarinet. Come on, gentlemen, sit down. Nobody uses this studio for a while." We each grabbed a chrome and gray plastic chair and sat. "OK," he said, "you play 'Saints' and what else?"

I looked at Lenny and Aaron. What a weird question. I thought he wanted to talk about Dr. Scharff and the flower, window and cat disaster.

" 'Twinkle,' " Lenny answered him. "We play 'Twinkle, Twinkle, Little Star.' "

"Far out," Leroi said with a half smile. He shook his head like it really pleased him somehow. "Who are you?"

"Lenny Barker. I play the comb."

Leroi stared at him and shook his head again. He looked over at Aaron. "And you're—"

"Aaron Colby, violin."

"Violin, comb and clarinet playing 'Twinkle, Twinkle, Little Star.' Well," he said, "it's just crazy enough to have possibilities." He put his elbows on the desk, his hands over his eyes, and sat there quiet for a minute or two like he was thinking hard. "I guess I can improvise around it. It's been done before." He said it out loud, but he wasn't talking to us. "*Better* something simple." Then he turned back and grinned again. "Get out your instruments and let's try something. You play what I tell you, OK?"

We looked at each other, wondering. I wasn't about to play "Twinkle" and then ask Leroi Rupert for money.

"It's all right," he said. "I just want to hear how you sound."

I took the mouthpiece off my clarinet and sucked on the reed, while Lenny folded some ragged waxed paper over the huge green comb and Aaron fumbled with his violin. Leroi Rupert leaned forward and watched us, smiling like the whole thing was good. Then he kind of looked off in the distance and began talking to himself again.

"OK, we'll start with a cart of a spaceship blast-off and segue into fireworks bursting in the air—just explode their eardrums—set off some smoke pots on the stage and then cut the sound altogether, absolutely quiet for . . . for about three seconds and then," he looked straight at us now, "then you start 'Little Star,' Aaron." Leroi pointed at him. Aaron looked puzzled, but he put the violin to his chin and played, without a mistake, all the way through "wonder what you are."

"Keep going, Aaron. Now, Fog, start at the beginning, like in a round." I blew "Twinkle, Twinkle," and as soon as I got to "what you are," he pointed to Lenny, who had the comb ready to go. Lenny's comb-humming knocked Leroi out. He howled and slapped his knee. "OK, OK, we'll make that good, hype it up through a phase-shifter, and my electric piano will pick it up and take off." He put his hands over his eyes again and then looked up and said, "You want to play that with me and a couple of high-school kids at the concert tomorrow night? I'll pay you enough to cover your debt to Dr. Scharff."

"No," Aaron answered, right away.

"Sure," Lenny said, almost drowning him out.

"No, we don't," Aaron went on. "Anyway, you know we're not good enough. You'd just be doing it to be nice to us . . . because you know we need the money."

"I'm doing it because it sounds good in my head. I want to hear how it sounds live. I'll tell you exactly why. You know I'm MC-ing this concert for the Park District tomorrow night. And they asked me if I'd play a number on the electric piano. And I said, 'Sure, no sweat,' but I haven't been able to settle on anything. Lots of things I *could* play. I got a drummer from Evanston High and a bass player from Skokie to back me up. They can do anything. They'll go along with 'Little Star.' And I like it."

He looked at all three of us and nodded his head like it was settled. *"Especially* you, Aaron," he said. "You'll give it class." Aaron hung his head and didn't say anything. "Come on, let's see how it ends." Leroi put his hands out wide like he was conducting an orchestra. "The electric piano wails and fades. I'll point to you, Comb, and you come in humming. Now, we'll do it the same way we did it at first, only in reverse order. Got it?'' Lenny started at the beginning and I joined him when Leroi pointed to me. ''Aaron, you're the last one. Start out loud and then at the end you make it disappear, like a falling star. That's it. You hold that last note. Make it a long fading line. Beautiful, beautiful starry night. That's good,'' he said. ''That's good.'' He folded his arms like that was that.

''Well, group, you've got to have a *name* to be a group, a name to catch the ear and dazzle the mind. What do you think?'' Leroi bit on a fingernail, thinking.

''A name?'' Aaron asked. ''Like we're *real?*''

''How about . . . ?'' But I couldn't think of a how about.

''How about the Debtors Three,'' Aaron said, with a sigh.

''Not *quite* enough glitter,'' Leroi told him. ''You need something snakey. You gotta *grab* 'em.''

''Like the backward scream does,'' Lenny said, and he tried to imitate it.

''You got it,'' Leroi said.

''Why not *that* then?'' I asked.

''Why not what?'' Aaron said.

''The Backward Screams!'' I shouted.

''The Backward Screams? *Fabulous!*'' Leroi yelled. ''You are genuine end-of-the-rainbow fans! And you are all right. I am glad to introduce to the world,'' and he bowed to us all, "the fantastic, the galactical Backward Screams!"

He slapped his hands on his legs, leaned forward and said, "Well, now, think your folks'll let you do it?"

"I don't know," I told him. I wasn't sure if they'd call it good experience or crazy. "Would . . . would *you* talk to them?" I asked. "I don't know if they'd exactly believe us."

"Glad to," he said. "By the way, have you guys said anything to your folks about your debt to Dr. Scharff?"

"Dr. Scharff makes me barf," Lenny said.

Leroi laughed.

"It's not funny," Lenny went on. "My mom and dad work for her. She's their boss."

"Then if she called me, it's a cinch she's already talked to them," Leroi said.

"Yeah, I've been thinking about that. That's probably why my mom was trying to find me this morning. 'Lenny, how *could* you!' my mom's gonna say. 'The whole *music* department's talking about you.' "

"Well, I didn't tell mine last night," Aaron said, "because Dr. Scharff said she'd give us till Friday without telling our folks. I thought just maybe we'd make it. I didn't want to tell them unless I *had* to."

"I guess that was before the cat went crazy on the curtain rod," Leroi said. " 'Two days in a row,' the lady yelled at me. 'They rang the bell on my precious, sensitive Fog *two days in a row.*' ''

"But we didn't!" Aaron shouted. "That's a lie. Today we were out scrounging money on the subway. She's got it all wrong. We really didn't ring it today."

Lenny turned all red, wheeled away, and walked over toward the control-room window with his head down. "OK, Aaron, *you* didn't," he said, turning around. "Listen, that Dr. Scharff makes me so mad. You know what she did last night? She called my dad and said that, unless I improve my lawn cutting and my *attitude,* she's gonna fire me. And my dad told me to shape up. My mom was mad, too, and she said what was I ever going to amount to if I wasn't even able to keep a simple job cutting grass." He dug the toe of his sneaker into the carpet.

"On the way to the train this morning I stopped and rang Dr. Scharff's bell about a billion times. She was at the university and the dogs were at the window, foaming. I wished it would blast that old cat right up the chimney. I didn't even care. I just did it."

8

You Couldn't Pay Me
to Do That

"The first thing we do," Leroi Rupert said as we rode down the elevator, "is to get over to Dr. Scharff's house before she explodes or calls the FBI."

"But what are we gonna do when we get there? She's gonna feed my toes to Beethoven, Brahms and Johann Sebastian Bark," Lenny said, sticking the waxed-papered comb into his back pocket.

"She's what?" Leroi Rupert asked.

"The dogs," Aaron explained. "Those are the names of her dogs."

"Listen, anybody who gives names like that to dogs can't be all bad," Leroi said.

"You'll see," Lenny told him. The door opened on the fourth floor and a couple of kids got on with their mother. They carried tooth-brushes some dental assistant had written their names on with a drill. They didn't even realize it was Leroi Rupert standing there in the elevator with them.

When we got off in the lobby, I asked him, "How come you don't talk like Leroi Rupert when you're not on the air?"

"Ah," he said, "that talk's for show, Fog. On the *one* hand, there's Leroi Rupert, DJ, fast-talkin' mystery cat, flashin' out bats and gargoyles through the radio waves and strikin' lightnin' through your veins with the—"

"Backward scream," I cut in.

"Named a famous trio after it!" He laughed. "But on the *other* hand, I don't scare my babies at home with the backward scream. That's a different world on the thirteenth floor. Can't ever start lettin' myself be like that off the air. I'd go bonkers."

"You'd go *bats,*" Lenny said, laughing.

"You bet your frosty blood, I would," Leroi Rupert said, laughing with him.

Aaron was staring at Leroi. "You really got *kids?*" he asked.

"Sure, two knockouts," he said. "Rosetta's five." And then he smiled like he was going to tell us a joke. "And we've got a son who's six weeks old." He looked at me and laughed. "We named him Leroi."

"Leroi Rupert?" I yelped. "There's a little Leroi Rupert?"

"Sure. That's how I happened to talk to your Dr. Scharff. Michelle called and said there was a doctor on the phone all excited, wanted to talk to me about my son Leroi. Like to scared me to death."

"I bet you were surprised to hear he was out busting flowerpots," Lenny said, laughing.

"You know it," Leroi said. "I thought he was sick or hurt. When I finally realized what was happening, the whole thing struck me as the funniest thing I'd ever heard. I laughed. She didn't."

As we passed the fountain in the lobby, Leroi dug his hand in his pocket and pulled out a penny. He flipped it into the fountain.

"What's that for?" Aaron asked him.

"For luck. I've got a feeling we're going to need it."

The bus outside took us to three blocks from Dr. Scharff's house. Leroi paid. "I'll put it on your expense account," he said. It seemed like a very short ride, and no matter how slow we walked from the bus stop, the space between us and her kept getting smaller.

As Lenny unlocked the gate with his key, we could hear the dogs in the front window ralphing again.

"They don't sound musical," Leroi Rupert said. "They sound like watchdogs."

"They look like killers," I told him.

"Same thing," he said, and rang the doorbell. The dogs barked louder.

"Geez!" Lenny yelled. "I don't believe it! You rang the doorbell!"

Leroi put his hand to his head and groaned. "I did it without thinking."

Dr. Scharff opened the door and glared at us through the screen. She was wearing a red Japanese-looking robe with dragons sewn on it in gold. The dogs stood there beside her, growling.

"What in heaven's name *is* this?" she demanded, throwing her head back. "Why did you ring my bell?"

Lenny tried a big smile. "Me and my friends have come to apologize and—"

"Do you think it's amusing? Invading my privacy?" Then she lowered her voice about two octaves and said dramatically, "I'm going to call the police. Sit," she told the dogs. They sat, and stopped growling, but their mouths were watering.

"Dr. Scharff," Leroi started out, sounding very patient. "We have come to pay you for the flowers and the broken glass."

"Are you that radio person I spoke with this morning?" she asked.

"The one and only," Leroi Rupert said with a sigh.

"Flies on his fleas, scabs on his knees, and braces on his splendid fangs," Lenny said, without smiling.

"You got a good memory, Comb," Leroi told him, giving him a light knuckle rub on the head.

"Dr. Scharff," I said, thinking maybe manners was what she wanted, "I want you to meet Leroi Rupert, the *real* Leroi Rupert, WOGR-AM. He's hired us to play in a concert with him so we can pay you."

"Then who are *you?*" she asked. Her eyes looked straight at me, cold as ice.

"Mitchell Ralph McDandel, 123-7643. My folks own Sunshine Health Food Store—if you want to rat on me." I was sorry as soon as I said it, but it made me so mad the way she stared at me like I was a criminal.

Lenny threw me a scared look and said, "We're all sorry about the window and the flowers and the pot . . . and about the cat."

"*Are* you?" she asked, like she didn't believe him. "Leonard," she said, "this has all been most unpleasant for me, and unpleasantness gives me headaches. I want you to know that I no longer require you to cut my lawn. This morning I hired a professional lawn service."

"They'll charge more than three dollars," Lenny said, and she gave him one of those laser-beam looks. She was a whole lot scarier than Leroi Rupert could ever be.

"They'll be worth more," she said.

"My dad says I've *got* to do it," Lenny went on.

"I'll talk with him about that," she said crisply. "If his teaching ability were anything

97

like your gardening ability, I'm sure he'd be out looking for work right now. I'd like my gate key now, if you please."

Lenny gulped. "I'm not so bad. I just don't cut grass good."

"What *do* you do well, Leonard?" she asked.

"I can play *Für Elise* by heart on the piano and I . . . I play the . . . comb, professionally," Lenny said, with a straight face.

Dr. Scharff closed her eyes and held out her hand for the key. Lenny dug it out of his pocket and gave it to her. One of the dogs growled.

Leroi pulled out his wallet and took out some bills. "You were just jivin' me a little when you told me you paid the vet twenty dollars for the cat's nerves, weren't you, Dr. Scharff?" he said.

Her face turned as red as her robe. "You didn't seem to realize the seriousness of the situation," she said sharply, "laughing like that."

"I thought so." He smiled, very nice, not sarcastic at all. "Kids aren't the only ones who stretch the truth to suit the circumstances." He gave her a little bow. "Well, we'd like to invite you to the jazz concert tomorrow night in Bennett Bowl. The boys here and I are going to play a few variations on 'Twinkle, Twinkle, Little Star.' "

"I am not fond of jazz," she said, "unless it is very well played." She opened the screen door to take the money. "Sit," she told the dogs, who were getting up on their haunches, ready to spring.

"Good-bye," we all said to her, and she closed the door tight. We could hear the chain lock snap into place.

After we walked out the front gate, we stood and looked back at the house.

"Well, now I don't need the key anymore," Lenny sighed, "—just like the bald-headed man."

"The bald-headed man?" I asked him, knowing, just knowing he was setting me up.

"Yeah," Lenny said, throwing me the punchline automatically. "*He* didn't need a key because he'd lost his locks."

Leroi was the only one who laughed. "Comb, you are one funny kid. You know any monster jokes?"

Lenny looked up at him and shook his head. "None about boys," he said, "but plenty about ghouls."

"Look," Leroi told him, "I'm always running short. Write me out the ones you know and I'll pay you a dollar for every one I use on the air."

"I know a million." Lenny brightened.

"Ah, but I don't *have* a million." Leroi smiled and turned to Aaron. "Aaron, how you doin'?" He must have noticed, too, that Aaron hadn't said a thing. He'd just stood there with his head down.

"Were you scared of her?" I asked him.

"No," he said, "*she* doesn't scare me. I was just thinking."

We decided to go talk to my folks at Sunshine first, since Aaron wasn't looking so good and Lenny didn't think his mom and dad would be home yet.

It was almost five, time for the last-minute crowd to be rushing in for the supper stuff they'd forgotten. But when we walked up, it looked like the shop was more jammed than usual. "Maybe we'd better wait," I said.

"I don't have that much time," Leroi Rupert told me. "I've got to get home, too."

We opened the door and went in. "Aaron!" somebody called. We looked over and saw Aaron's mom coming over to him. "Where've you boys been? And what's this about you damaging somebody's property? I can't believe it."

"Not just *anybody*'s property, either." Lenny's father was there, and his mom, too.

"Let's all go back to the office," Dad said, "and find out what this is all about." He turned and saw Leroi Rupert standing at his elbow. "Well, hello," he said to him. "*More* peanut butter? Your wife and kids were in this afternoon and bought a quart."

"No," Leroi answered. "No peanut butter this time. I came in with Mitchell." He shook hands with my father. "I think we've never officially met. I'm Leroi Rupert, a disc jockey on WOGR.'' My mom looked up from the alfalfa sprouts she was ringing up for a man in jogging shorts.

"You're Leroi Rupert?" she said. "No kidding!" He smiled at her, glad she knew who he was.

"Hurry it up, lady," the jogger said. "This place is like the subway at rush hour."

"The boys have quite a story to tell you," Leroi told my dad.

All the parents started talking at once to us and to Leroi as we started back to the office. They'd been at the store fifteen minutes already, trying to figure the whole thing out and trying to find out where we'd gone. Lenny's folks and Aaron's mother had both gotten calls from Dr. Scharff and, since nobody had heard from us by four o'clock, they'd gathered at Sunshine for a council of war.

"I'm surprised at you, Mitch," my father said. "We'll put those idle hands to work next week in the stockroom. I'd have thought you could handle a month of freedom better than that."

"I don't know what we're going to do with you, Lenny," his mom said. It sounded like a sweaty stockroom didn't sound bad enough to her. "Dr. Scharff is hard enough to get along with without this. I hope she doesn't just wash her hands of the whole family."

Lenny looked at me. From his face, I could tell that it was probably the first time he had ever really panicked.

"Oh, Linda," Lenny's dad said. "She's not that bad. Granted she was mad at Lenny. . . ." He turned to the rest of us. "You've got to understand about Dr. Scharff." Lenny and I sat down on a wood crate. Aaron stood over by his mom, looking down at the floor.

"Alvina Scharff was an opera singer years ago," Lenny's dad went on, "when it was fashionable to be a prima donna—grand, dramatic and temperamental. When her voice was no longer strong, she came to the university as a teacher and then more or less bullied her way to the head of the department. She frightens her students at first with her flamboyance, but let me tell you that classy lady doesn't settle for anything a whit less than excellent. That's what's made our music department as fine as it is."

"She doesn't think I'm excellent," Lenny said. He looked at me again and turned a kind of yellow-green. *"I'm* afraid of her."

"If you ask me, she seems pretty afraid herself," Leroi said. "Do you know how many locks she has on her door? And those dogs? In any case, I think the boys have set things right with her."

Nobody heaved a sigh of relief.

"I expect you'd better hear what happened," Leroi said, turning to me.

I told the story mostly. But Lenny couldn't help adding the things I left out on purpose, like our getting out of the subway where all the bars were and about how we lost the money between the cars.

And then Leroi Rupert took over and told his part. When we were all finished, Aaron's mother said, "I can't believe it. Aaron is such a quiet boy." She gave him a hug. "It was *his* idea to perform on the train?"

"He suggested it," I told her. "Right, Aaron?" He didn't say anything. "But he wasn't so hot for the idea once we got started."

"You know," she said, looking around at all the other parents, "Aaron wouldn't even play in the spring concert at school. 'It's just stage fright,' I told him. 'Everybody gets it sometimes.'"

Aaron looked at her and said, "I'm not going to play tomorrow night either." He turned to us. "I just can't. The more I think about it, the more I know I can't do it."

I knew Aaron was scared, but I didn't think he'd let us down like that. Leroi had already given Dr. Scharff the money. He was counting on us.

But Aaron had been quiet so long, he just couldn't stop talking. "It was awful on that subway. It made my stomach turn inside out. The only reason I did it then was we had to get the money. That and its being my idea and all. I'm sorry, Mr. Rupert," he said. "I don't know how fast I can get the money to pay you back for what you gave Dr. Scharff. I'll baby-sit every night and I'll collect empty bottles. . . . But you just couldn't *pay* me to play tomorrow night. All those people in the audience staring and laughing at me."

"Aaron," Leroi said, all calm. "It wouldn't be the same without you—that cool, clear violin. You sure do play it well. You *like* to play, don't you?"

"Yes, I do, but—"

"Tell you what. What if I have them dim the lights so everybody will be looking up at the stars, not at you? And I'll cut out all the phony sound effects at the very beginning and we'll just play your part straight. No comedy routine. No razzmatazz. I promise, nobody will laugh at you."

"Come on, Aaron," Lenny begged him. "What's a comb and a clarinet sound like? Nothing."

"Not exactly *nothing*," I said. "Look, if we lived through that subway ride, we can make it through this concert."

"Aaron," his mother said to him, "your father and I would love to hear you play tomorrow night. It would make us proud."

"I decided not to," Aaron said, all quiet.

"Well," Lenny declared grandly, "you can change your mind! People do that all the time." He grabbed Aaron's arm. "If you think they'll laugh at you because of me playing the green plastic comb, *I'll* drop out so you can play. What do you think of that?''

"I think you don't get off that easy," Aaron said, smiling weakly.

"You'll do it then?" Leroi asked.

"If you promise it'll be dark and nobody will laugh."

"May diving bats carry me off by my monster nose if they do!" Leroi declared. "I have to leave. See you all in the Bowl tomorrow night at seven. You'll be fantastic!"

9

The Backward Screams

By seven o'clock the seats in Bennett Bowl were beginning to fill up. Even with the sun low, it was still hot, and lots of people were sitting on blankets in the grass, eating and waiting for the concert to start. There were loudspeakers in the trees, and when the music started you could hear it all over the lawn outside the Bowl. My folks and me picnicked there sometimes on Friday evenings. When I was little, my mom used to bring books for me to look at and a blanket for when I got sleepy, and then my dad would carry me back to the car after the concert was over.

We could see the high-school bands gathering and hear little bits and pieces of the music they were going to play. And there was Leroi Rupert on the stage, waving his hands and giving directions. He wore the monster hat, its long warty nose curled over his left ear. The shiny red, green and pink suit he wore matched the colors in the monster hat. It was gruesome. A gang of kids hung around the edge of the stage, holding up things to be autographed. He kneeled down and started to sign.

Somebody blew into a microphone. "Testing. Testing. One-two-three-four. This-is-some-bore." Then she went on to the next mike. There were five mikes set across the stage. One of them didn't make a sound, so she hopped off and headed for a truck full of equipment.

Leroi saw us and motioned to us to come on down.

We were a crowd all by ourselves. There were eleven of us. Dad had brought us all in the van. There were Mom and Dad and me, Mr. and Mrs. Barker with Lenny and Miriam, and Mr. and Mrs. Colby, Aaron and Lucille. Our parents had wanted us to dress up, but Lenny and Aaron and me all wore jeans and our old *WOGR—IT'S A SCREAM!* T-shirts. We thought Leroi would like that.

As we walked down the big stone steps of the Bowl, it felt like everybody sitting on the long wooden benches was staring at us like they knew we were going to perform. But they weren't. They were talking to each other or pointing down toward the bands, trying to find somebody they knew.

"They're going to have a big crowd here all right," Lenny's dad said. "It'll be filled to overflow if just the parents of all those high-school kids show up." A guy with a trumpet stepped up to the dead microphone.

"Try it, will you?" the lady in the sound truck yelled. He held the horn up high and blew. The mike snapped on right in the middle of a high note and a lot of people on the lawn must have dropped their fried chicken. "He's good," Lenny's dad said. "He's really good. Say, Len, how about starting off with a trumpet in the fall?" Lenny shrugged his shoulders.

"Do I *have* to watch?" Lucille whined. Aaron's mother leaned down over her and whispered, "Didn't Aaron blow you a nice blue balloon poodle this afternoon?"

"It broke," Lucille said. "Besides," she went on, staring down at Leroi Rupert, "I wanta go home."

"I'll lay out the blanket and play with her in the grass," Miriam said, taking Lucille by the hand. "Come on, Lucy, I'll tell you about this little girl whose room was filled with blue balloons and the whole place, wallpaper and all, floated up into the sky." They started back up the steps.

"What's her name?" Lucille asked.

"What do you think?"

"I think it's Lucille and I don't like that story."

The Morton High Band was on the stage ready to go. Leroi came over and said hello to our folks. "Can't be seen shaking hands," he said. "It's bad for the image. Not crazy enough. I could try a handstand."

"Hello's just fine," Aaron's dad said. "Our four-year-old daughter took one look at your extra nose and retreated to her blanket."

Leroi reached up and pulled his monster hat down farther over his eye. He looked pleased that he'd scared somebody. "We saved seats for you in the front row. You grab them now and I'll show these stars the stage," he said.

A line of tall pine trees took the place of curtains at the back of the big stone-and-concrete platform. They didn't quite hide the other two bands that were back there last-minute practicing.

"Aaron," Leroi called, "you take the middle mike. Fog, you stand at the mike to the right of him. Comb on the left." The sound lady came over and pulled the microphones down. "You know for certain what we're going to do?" We knew. We should have. The three of us had been practicing all day.

"And in between, when you're not playing, just look at the holes in the toes of your sneakers or at the audience or at the guy who's playing," Leroi explained. "But keep an eye on me, if you think it might be your turn. Most of all, enjoy it. You OK, Aaron?" Aaron looked grim, but he nodded. "Questions?" We shook our heads. "OK, then go settle yourselves in the front row, watch the show, and clap as loud as you can."

The bands were pretty good, I guess. Everybody clapped a lot for them. And Leroi made the whole crowd break up between songs with his spacey monster talk and crazy effects from the sound truck. But the three of us kept shifting around, wondering when it was going to be time. I had my fingers crossed that Aaron would make it to the stage at all. He was just staring at the violin on his lap. I'd been sucking my clarinet reed to keep it damp. Lenny was playing with the big green comb, bending it back and forth.

I glanced back at the audience, rows and rows of heads, nodding to each other and to the beat of the music. Every once in a while, I'd see a face I knew from school or from the store and I'd feel a twist in my stomach.

As my eyes skipped past the rows on the far side of the Bowl, they suddenly stopped at a head of red hair I'd have known anywhere. "Lenny!" I yelped, and I grabbed his arm. He looked up, puzzled, and I pointed my clarinet. "Fifth row up," I said. "Near the aisle."

"Geez," he breathed. And he snapped the comb in two.

Aaron heard the crack. "You crazy or something?" he whispered. "How you gonna play with a broken comb?"

"Forget it. I can't play anyway," Lenny said, tossing the pieces on the ground and pointing over to Dr. Scarff. "Dr. Frankenstein sees me stand up and play a comb, and she's gonna say I'm stinking up the reputation of her music department or something. She'll fire my dad for sure." He bent his head down over his knees.

"Look," I told him, shaking his elbow back and forth. "She already knows you're playing. You don't want her to think you're a chicken, do you?"

"Can't you boys be quiet?" Lenny's mom said, leaning over to us. "I'm trying to listen."

"Lenny's right. Let's forget it," Aaron whispered. "Leroi Rupert doesn't need us. We're nothing. He's got three big bands back there."

I looked over at the stage where the conductor was whipping his arms back and forth like he was trying to clear the air of a million mosquitoes. The music was getting louder and louder and louder. Then, all at once, he dropped his hands to his sides and the music stopped. It was really worth a big hand, but I wasn't up to it. All three of us sat there like wet winter coats.

"And that," Leroi Rupert announced, "was Thad Jones' 'Big Dipper,' poured on you cool for a hot night by the Evanston High Jazz Band." Everybody in the band got up and bowed, and then picked up their chairs and moved them back so some guys could carry a lot of big pots onto the stage.

"I've got some young friends here tonight," Leroi Rupert began. He looked down at the front row and motioned us up.

"All right, stay. I'm going," I said, and without looking back I stalked off alone toward the stage.

"Wait up," Aaron called, and I could hear him following me.

"Anybody got a comb?" Lenny yelled. "Mine just broke."

"I've got a rat-tail one here somewhere. That OK?" his mother asked.

We trailed onto the stage with all the whoop-ee of three guys going to the dentist.

"We're gonna fool around," Leroi was saying, "with a piece about just one of those glittering stars out there in the universe." He raised both his hands high and looked up. The audience looked up, too. The stage lights dimmed down to nothing until it was almost all dark, and you could see the stars up there as bright and clear as they ever get this close to the city. I could just make out Leroi as he grabbed his monster hat by the nose and flung it back toward the band. Then his voice changed and he stopped being Leroi Rupert, crazy DJ, and started sounding more like Mister Leroi Rupert.

"We're going to celebrate those stars up there with a melody that's centuries old. You've all known it since you were kids. Mozart wrote a set of variations on the tune for the piano. We're going to do our own twentieth century version tonight, with a new young group called the Backward Screams—Mitch McDandel on clarinet, Aaron Colby playing violin, and Leonard Barker humming the comb."

I could see Lenny's outline across the stage. He shrugged his shoulders as if to say, "Why not?"

"Blake Sidell at the drums and John Ryan, bass, will back us up, and I'll take my turn on the electric piano." He waited about half a minute till it was very quiet. " 'Little Star,' " he announced, and he gave a deep bow toward Aaron.

Everything was still and dark and I kept thinking about Leroi Rupert saying, "I promise, nobody will laugh at you." But I knew they'd laugh, if we played bad. Aaron must have known it, too. There wasn't anything Leroi could do about that. Even the picnickers were quiet, though, lying there like I used to, looking up at the stars, watching for meteors and satellites.

My knees were weak. Aaron was so scared I could feel it. I couldn't say, "It's OK" or "You'll be great" because the mikes were on. I saw him take a deep breath and step up to his center mike. The audience was still quiet, but he didn't look at them once. He just propped the violin under his chin and started to play. Very slow but very clear. It sounded

whistle of fireworks and the blast of a
gong off. It was fabulous!

good in the dark. Lenny was at the other side of the stage, shifting back and forth from one foot to the other and trying to get the waxed paper to fit his new comb with a handle. I held the clarinet up to my lips, waiting for the signal. The reed was practically waterlogged. When Leroi pointed at me, though, I started. A note squeaked bad and I could have died. Leroi nodded, and Lenny started humming and vibrating. He bounced and swayed as he played. When he finished, we got a good burst of applause. Aaron smiled.

Then Leroi Rupert's electric piano started up. I'd never heard him play before. He played the piano like Leroi Rupert, DJ, fast and fancy. When he slid his thumb down the keys, it was like a whole shower of stars.

Aaron looked up at him and grinned. "Way to go, Leroi," he called. The mike caught his voice and broadcast it to the crowd. Everybody clapped and yelled in the dark.

"Way to go, Screams," Leroi yelled back and blasted out a huge chord on the electric piano. It was as if that chord was an electric switch. All at once four red and blue smoke pots exploded on stage, covering the place with fog, and a whole set of strobe lights started flashing off and on and off and on. From the loudspeakers you could hear the long thin whistle of fireworks and the blast of rockets going off. It was fabulous!

The audience went wild. The whole place flashed and blasted and whirled for about five minutes while Leroi wove our song around so that half the time you thought he'd forgotten what he was playing. Before long, though, you'd hear the tune sneak in again and off he'd go. I saw him nod to the sound-truck lady and the blast of a spaceship came careening out of the speakers. The lights snapped on and Leroi pointed to the drummer. Just as the spaceship seemed to hit orbit, the drummer started his solo, *pow-pow-crash-riffle-pow-bam*. The audience yelled again. Then the bass player had his turn going *BOOM-boom-boom-boom-BOOM-boom-be-boom-boom*. It was wild!

Leroi played again and then pointed at Lenny, but Lenny wasn't even looking at him. He was standing there, staring out at the audience toward Dr. Scharff's seat. I looked over, too. The seat was empty.

Leroi finally had to yell, "Hey, Comb, go!" Lenny looked over, startled, and got a laugh. I guess he didn't mind, though, because he started clowning it up. Right in the middle of his part, he stuck in a chorus of "Oh she wore green pants to the hoochie-koochie dance and the pants she wore cost a dollar ninety-four." The audience loved it.

I wasn't gonna have Leroi shout "Clarinet" or "Fog" at me, though. I came in right on cue. I didn't hit a bad note this time, but I think I wasn't remarkable either. Nobody whooped, and I could tell my folks were the loudest clappers in the place.

Aaron came in when he was supposed to, too. And he didn't look like an icicle this time, either. He was smiling a little when he played, "like a diamond in the sky," as sweet and clear as Leroi had told him to. And when it was all over, the audience clapped again, only a little of it for us, I think. Most of it was for Leroi Rupert and the lights and sounds.

Leroi stepped forward. "Thank you, thank you," he said. He pointed to the drummer and the bass player. They bowed. He pointed to us, "And the Backward Screams." We sort of bowed. Lenny just shrugged his shoulders.

The lights turned low with a spotlight trained on Leroi Rupert, who was wearing his funny hat again. "Gaze," he commanded, pointing up to the sky, "past the stars. Where the cow . . . jumps over the moon!" And a fabulous sound washed out over us all. It was the sound of a cow—mooing backward! Everybody laughed. It had been a good night and I felt wonderful, like I'd just eaten a really great meal.

"And now it's time and space," Leroi said, "to blast off to wherever your home might be. Good night." The spotlight snapped off, a smoke pot in front of him exploded, and when all the lights turned on again, Leroi Rupert had disappeared.

"Oh, no," this kid in front of me groaned.

He'd come down with a big sheet of paper to get Leroi Rupert's autograph.

We climbed off the stage feeling pretty smug.

A bald guy with glasses turned to the kid with him. "I don't know why you dragged me out here," he said. "It was just a buncha noise."

Lenny started to laugh. "At least we know they heard us," he said. We started off to our seats.

It was then we saw that Leroi Rupert was the only one who had disappeared. There, standing next to Lenny's folks, was Dr. Scharff. She was wearing this pink lacy shawl with long, long fringes. It didn't look like they were having a party, though. She was filling their ears about something, shaking her finger at Mr. Barker. Lenny stopped cold. "I told you I shouldn't have done it," he said.

Dr. Scharff looked up. "Leonard," she called sternly, "I was just telling your parents. You must learn to bow properly. A shrug won't do."

"How did you like it?" I asked her.

She looked the three of us over. "The high-school bands, I thought, were quite good," she said. "As for the rest," and she waved her hand, "as show business, it was first-rate. As music, well, it was *A* for effort, but worth something less than thirty dollars."

Lenny put the comb to his mouth and played another fanfare.

"May we take you home?" my dad asked Dr. Scharff.

"Certainly not," she said, grand as a duchess. "I have my car." And she swept off into the night.

"Well," Dad went on, "what do you boys plan for an encore?"

"Plenty," I told him. "We're gonna get up at five o'clock tomorrow and fish all morning off the end of the pier."

"I do hope," my mom said, "you use those chilled worms in the refrigerator. I was afraid you planned to serve them in a salad for supper."

Everybody laughed, like that would have been a super dumb idea. But we found out that hot summertime fish really like those cold worms. Before eight o'clock next morning, we caught four big ones. There was one for the Barkers, one for the Colbys, one for my family, and one for the very best DJ of them all, the almost one-and-only Leroi Rupert.

ABOUT THE AUTHOR

JAMIE GILSON used her experience on an FM radio station to write *Dial Leroi Rupert, DJ*. She describes the fictitious world of WOGR as a zany variation on its real-life counterpart.

An energetic person, Ms. Gilson spends much of her time working with children. She lectures and holds children's writing and poetry workshops in the Chicago area, and also writes freelance for *Chicago* magazine. She and her husband, Jerome, have three children, one of whom is an accomplished musician.

Archway also plans to publish *Do Bananas Chew Gum?* by Jamie Gilson.

ABOUT THE ARTIST

JOHN WALLNER holds degrees from Washington University and the Pratt Institute, and has earned a reputation as a top children's book illustrator. He was recently named Best Juvenile Illustrator by the friends of American Writers and has been published in many award-winning children's books.